CASTEBOOK
ZENITH™

By Steve Kenson and David Wendt, Ph.D.

THE WAR WITH THE RATS

I am Huzok, and I owe my life to the Unconquered Sun.

My story begins like so many told to youngsters around the campfire. Only mine is not merely a tale to frighten children into behaving, but one of actual events, one of death and life.

It was the night of a dark moon, and the hills were thick with fog. Through the thick fog, a haunting melody played — an eerie piping that grew closer and closer to our small village. The young and the old were safe in their beds, and only the guards remained awake and about that night. The weird music grew louder until the stranger entered our village. His skin was pale. I had little trouble imagining that his skin had not seen the sun's warming rays in many years. He played a flute that appeared to be carved from bone. His black buff jacket was decorated with silver tracing, and he moved with a fluid grace. Yes, alas, I had the misfortune to be on guard duty that night.

The night visitor made no aggressive overtures, so I merely stood my post, watching carefully as he passed. He paused in his playing to give me a nod, which now, in remembrance, gives me a chill. Our village had a tradition dating back to the First Age of offering succor to travelers. I would not be the one to break that custom.

My fellows, however, were not so respectful of tradition. The other guards readied their spears and followed the stranger as he made his way through our town. Though aware of them, the pale one paid them no heed. He walked directly toward the nearest home. Putting away his pipe, he approached and knocked, bearing himself as if nobility. Curious, I left my post to watch. The master of the house only opened his door wide enough to turn the stranger away.

The knocking and the refusal were repeated at only a few more homes before my fellow guards gathered their nerve. Werul reached down for a fist-sized stone, gesturing to the others to join him. As the stranger prepared to disrupt the sleep of yet another family, they began to pelt him with the stones, without word or warning.

The pale visitor turned to face his attackers. For a moment, I was filled with overwhelming dread. The others paused in their attack, unwilling or unable to continue while his gaze was upon them. But rather than return violence upon the violent, the stranger merely took out his pipe and began to play as he walked calmly from our village.

My fellow guards congratulated themselves on their bravery, thinking that they had seen the last of the stranger. If only that had proved true.

* * * * *

Nothing more was heard of the weird piping for an entire month, and the episode was forgotten. We live in strange times, and our old ones tell of even stranger times past. However, when the dark moon crested the following month, the piping was heard once more over the hills. The guards, emboldened by their previous success, stood brazenly, waiting for the piper. As the music neared the village, we realized an unearthly counter point accompanied it, the chattering and squeaking of rodents.

The melody and its unearthly harmony drew closer and closer. Through the night fog they came, rats the size of wild boars. I drew my weapon to stave off the beasts, but fear held me otherwise near paralyzed. I watched as they fell upon the guards who had attacked the midnight visitor. I watched as the piper appeared in the parting fog, observing the rats and playing his strange song. I peered in abject horror at the beasts, noting their earthy stench and the old open wounds around which all manner of night insects swarmed.

The attack was shorter than the musical warning. The rats pulled down one of the guards and dragged him screaming into the darkness. As control returned to my muscles, I was struck that the rodents had paid me no heed.

The midnight attacks came nightly after that. The piper would direct his minions against the guards who had attacked him or against the homes that had denied him rest. Each night, the village would lose more men, and each night, the beasts would seem stronger. Finally, the village elder summoned me. "You alone remembered our tradition, you must be the one to save us," spoke the old woman.

"But what can I do? Our weapons are harmless against the beasts."

"You must find one whose weapons can harm the night visitor and his monsters."

"But who could stand against him? Do I seek a warrior? A priest? A god?"

"All of these things, and none. Let the sun be your guide."

* * * * *

And so, that is what I did. I traveled from dawn, walking toward the sun, until noon, when the sun was directly overhead. I rested then, only to start again in the afternoon, walking with the sun at my back, until sunset. I slept at night, only to begin again when the sun's first rays woke me.

I walked for three days and slept for three nights, and I began to despair that I would return too late, that my village would be empty by the time I could bring aid. On the fourth day, I set off again, walking toward the sun. It was nearly noon when I came across a battle. I stopped atop a hill and peered down at the two forces locked in combat. On one side were barbarians, clearly hardened by many battles. On the other were what seemed to be simple farmers, wielding hoes and forks. I watched in amazement as the peasants took the upper hand. They were organized and effective, and the barbarians faltered against them. I wondered how this could be, until I laid eyes upon their leader, a woman in red enamel armor, surrounded by the blazing white-gold light of the sun. She took the fight to the enemy's leader, and he fell before her, prompting the barbarians to flee. The battle was over before the sun began its downward journey through the sky.

I followed the victorious "army" as its members returned to their homes, catching the leader along the way. I told her my tale and the tale of my village, and she agreed to come with me.

* * * * *

The journey, so ponderous at the start, seemed somehow easier in the returning. The mere presence of the warrior, who named herself Karal Fire Orchid, eased my heart and lightened my step. What had originally taken three days took just over two, and we arrived in my village before the zenith of the seventh day following my departure.

The townsfolk approached Fire Orchid cautiously, with disbelief in their eyes. "We sent you for help, and you bring us this old woman?" I had noted that Karal's features were aged, but her strength and speed were that of a youth, and so, I had not paid any attention to her age. I was about to speak in her defense, when the warrior silenced me.

"What did you expect?" Karal spoke with a confidence and anger that silenced the crowd. "Did you expect me to bring my Circle to aid a village inhospitable to travelers? Did you expect a Seventh Legion field force to protect a town of oathbreakers and stone-throwers? Huzok told me your tale, and I have brought all that I need to aid you. However, if you doubt me, I can be gone by nightfall. Doubtless, your heroic menfolk will soon deal with the problem."

There was some murmuring from the crowd, but my fellows soon agreed that Fire Orchid was hero enough for the job.

The red-clad warrior set right to her task. She selected volunteers to be her aides. Some were to lead guard groups. Others were to run messages or gather supplies. One was to draw a map of the town, marking it as she directed. And as for myself, I was to be her second-in-command.

We walked the town, Karal's chosen scribe marking the location of buildings and where fortifications were to be built. At her direction, I supervised the construction of walls that would force the enemy to attack only where we allowed. Fire Orchid inspected what weapons and armor we had available and directed several townsfolk to construct additional armament from our available supplies. She taught her chosen leaders weapon maneuvers and sent them to teach their men. Some learned faster than others, and they were made unit leaders. I walked the town as the men drilled, helping where I could.

The village worked hard that afternoon, and while all was not complete when the sun set, Fire Orchid seemed pleased. "This war will not be won in a single battle, but we shall be ready for the battle that comes tonight." We all rested, and we ate, gathering what strength we could for the conflict we knew would come that night.

When the moon reached its height, we heard the music we had been dreading. Fire Orchid sent her runners to alert those who were guarding the fortifications. I stood at her side as she readied the troops she had picked to guard the only access into the town. I had not understood her choices at first. Those that stood were neither the best warriors in our town, nor the best armed, but as she spoke to them that night, I began to understand. Her forehead glowed with the mark of the Unconquered Sun as she spoke, and those gathered there seemed to gain strength from her words. They stood straighter, more confident and seemed to hold their weapons with greater skill. Even I was affected; the music that had previously filled me with such dread could find no purchase in my heart with Fire Orchid as my leader.

Runners came with reports as we waited. The great rats were hurling themselves against the battlements, but the walls constructed at Karal's orders stood against the tide. After each failure, the rodents moved onward, slowly circling the town, seeking entrance. It would not be long before they reached the opening that we guarded so diligently, and we knew what to do. Our forces at this gate were split into three groups. The first would control access to the town and would only let the rodents through two at a time. The other two groups would corral the beasts. Fire Orchid had given me a blade that she said would cut the creatures. She and I would cleave the heads from the cornered rats, and the process would begin anew.

And so it went. The rodents finally reached the entrance where we lay in wait. The rats were let through two by two, and we struck them down. A dozen lay, lifeless, destroyed by either Karal's sword or mine, before the night visitor retreated into the fog, taking his remaining forces with him. Fire Orchid announced that they would not return that night and sent us to rest for the morrow. As I drifted off, choosing to sleep in a pile of hay near the entrance, I saw that the warrior did not prepare to sleep herself.

* * * * *

I rose early the next morning and found piles of ash where the corpses had been left the night before. Fire Orchid was performing an elaborate kata in the light of the rising sun, a weapon drill I knew to be of the Seventh Legion fighting style. I watched as she completed her exercises, and together, we waited for the rest of the town to wake.

Once the rest of the town had stirred, we began again. The defenses were reinforced, the men continued to train, and Fire Orchid began to discuss strategy with her chosen lieutenants and myself. Discussion is not the right term. She outlined how we could defeat the rats and defend ourselves against even greater dangers, and we listened raptly, enthralled by her words.

When night came, we drove off another attack by the piper and his pets, and the next day, we continued to train. This cycle continued for three nights, but as we trained during the fourth day, Fire Orchid changed our orders.

"You have learned all you can from me. Tonight, we face the master of the rats, the pale musician. Tonight, we win the war."

Karal must have sensed the impatience of the town. The villagers had been pleased by their success, but they had wanted the piper defeated, not merely the monstrous rats. With her announcement, morale improved to its highest point yet.

That night, only one rat would be let through the gates at a time. Half of the guards would hold the entrance, while half would hold down each beast for me to slay. Meanwhile, Fire Orchid would stride into the night, to face the pale visitor who was at the heart of the matter. "Remove the capstone, and the house will fall."

As the sun set, the village was on fire with anticipation. As with previous nights, the great rodents tried their might against the barricades, and as with previous nights, their efforts failed. One by one, the guard posts reported in, as the beasts made their way around the city. Soon, they would attack the front gate, and we would be waiting for them. In retrospect, I can see how overconfident we were.

At first, all went as planned. The monsters attacked, and a single creature was allowed through. My troops pinned it down, and I moved in to cut it down.

Meanwhile, Fire Orchid strode into the night, her form blazing with the sun's golden light. The mass of great rats parted before her, burned by her touch, as she made her way toward the piper. The sea of rodents closed behind her, cutting us off from our protector, but not from her light.

We allowed a second rodent through, and I removed its head as easily as I had removed the head of the first.

As the hero reached her prey, the tune of the piping changed. It swelled to a shrieking attack anthem and, then, stopped suddenly. The rats surged forward, surprising and overwhelming the guards that stood with me at the gate. I sent runners for reinforcements, but I feared that many would fall before this latest onslaught.

I strode forward to join the fray, striking at the monsters with the sword Fire Orchid had gifted me. When I could, I peered toward her golden light, to observe her progress.

Golden sparks filled the sky, accented with dimmer, less frequent silver ones. In occasional flashes of brilliance, I could see our champion clearly. In some, she struggled beneath the pale man's assault, but in more, she held the upper hand.

It was in attempting to observe her battle that I made a grave mistake. Sensing my distraction from the fight, one of the great rats leapt upon me, knocking the sword from my hand and pinning me beneath its weight. I could feel its fetid breath upon me. It clawed at my chest, opening wounds that I knew even then were destined to scar, if I were fortunate enough to survive. I sensed my life ebbing away, fleeing before the mere presence of the monster. Then the sky flared.

I was told later that Fire Orchid had been engulfed in a great plume of light reminiscent of her namesake. While so surrounded, she struck down the pale piper. In the instants that followed, golden flame chased silver lightning as it raced across the landscape. Wherever one of the great rats stood, the two energies converged, and the beast was consumed. I saw the light, felt the heat and fell into unwilling sleep.

* * * * *

When I woke, I was told that Fire Orchid had gone. She had left the sword that she had lent me and recommended that my village appoint me leader. The people took her advice, and to this very day, I use that blade to defend them.

I am Huzok, and I owe my life to the Unconquered Sun.

Credits

Authors: Steve Kenson and David Wendt, Ph.D.
Storyteller Game System Design: Mark Rein•Hagen
Developer: Geoffrey C. Grabowski
Editor: John Chambers
Art Direction: Brian Glass
Artists: Sanford Greene, Wendy Grieb, Janeen Satone, Chris Stevens and E.J. Su
Cover Art: Melissa Uran
Cover Design: Brian Glass
Layout and Typesetting: Brian Glass

Special Thanks:

Steve "Thump Thump Thump" Wieck, for summing up how we all felt on the last day of GenCon.
Rich "Look At It Burn!" Thomas, for sharing an important lesson about drinking.
Conrad "Lightweight" Hubbard, for not telling me it was a drinking contest. Sorry about that, Conrad.
Tim "Playing With His Food" Avers, for an excellent impression of someone who didn't really want that dinner.
Ramsey "Grrr" Blair, for all the many happy hours we spend together on our days off.
Also, special thanks to Angel; Mike Lee; Tammy, Ray and the rest of the Wolfpack demo team staff; Bill Wulf; Amul Kumar; Marichristine Storch; Oliver and Ollie; the poor bartender at the Milwaukee Airport; the structural engineer I talked with on the plane ride home; and anybody else who helped me stumble through GenCon 2001 with my head mostly still screwed on.

White Wolf Game Studio

735 Park North Blvd.
Suite 128
Clarkston, GA 30021
USA

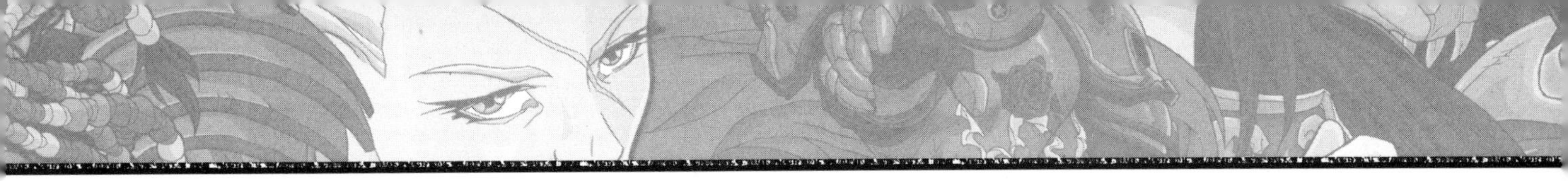

CASTE BOOK ZENITH™

TABLE OF CONTENTS

Introduction

Prophet, rouse the faithful to arms. If there are twenty steadfast men among you, they shall vanquish two hundred; and if there are a hundred, they shall rout a thousand unbelievers, for the infidel are devoid of understanding.
—The Meaning of the Qu'ran, 8:65

Caste Book: Zenith is a sourcebook to help you better understand the Zenith Caste Exalted and their place in the world of **Exalted**. The Zeniths, now most commonly known as the Blasphemous, blaze with the full light of the Unconquered Sun. They are the leaders and the priests and the seers of the First Age, and their return could herald the beginning of a righteous new era. Yet, their return might also serve only to illuminate the gradual but irreversible decline of the world into darkness and decadence. The Blasphemous are priests and leaders, but more than that, they are passionate, righteous lights in a dark world. They are master speakers and hardy survivors, but each is an individual on a unique mission for the Unconquered Sun. They are the Hammers of Heaven, the Chosen of the Sun. This book will help you to understand the varied members of this Caste, both before and after Exaltation. It also contains a number of new Charms and wonders to assist Zenith Caste Exalted in their crusade for justice.

To fully understand the Zenith Caste Exalted, you will need to understand the world in which they live, as well as the attitudes and natures of the other powerful beings with whom they interact. The warrior-priests of the Zenith come into a world that has been taught to loathe and fear their kind. This troubled time is filled with hostile Dragon-Blooded, Wyld-touched barbarians, eldritch Fair Folk, devious spirits and macabre Abyssal Exalted. **Caste Book: Zenith** describes some of the ways the newly reborn Zenith Caste Exalted feel about those with whom they share their world and how other powerful and dangerous entities view the return of the Zenith Caste.

In addition, the Zenith Caste is merely one of the five castes of Solar Exalted. Many Solar Exalted are drawn together into Circles made up of members of several castes. In these pages, you will learn how the Zenith Caste views its fellow Anathema, and how these various individuals feel about the righteously passionate Zenith Caste.

Each Zenith Caste Exalted is a uniquely powerful individual, gifted by the Unconquered Sun with unprecedented oratory ability and survival skills. However, they all share certain drives and imperatives. Only individuals who carry within them the potential to be truly influential missionaries and leaders can become members of the Zenith Caste. Once chosen by the Unconquered Sun, these individuals gain access to powerful Charms and visions of the First Age, which shape their centuries-long lives.

How to Use This Book

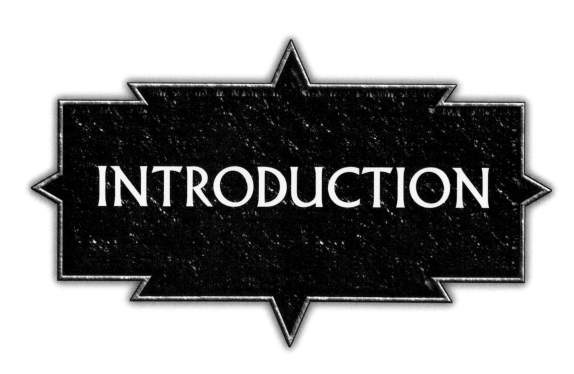

Caste Book: Zenith grants new insights into the lives and motives of the Zenith Caste. It also offers new powers and magical items for use by Zenith Caste Exalted. This book can help you better understand your character and her place in Creation, as well as offer information on how others in the world of **Exalted** are likely to react to your character. Players and Storytellers can also choose to ignore much of this book, picking and choosing the concepts, characters and situations that fit best in their series.

Chapter One: Our Souls Through Our Eyes introduces five very different Zenith Caste Exalted, describing in their own voices who they are and how they came to be Exalted. These characters provide examples of some of the diverse individuals who belong to this caste.

Chapter Two: Obligations of the Caste provides a range of opinions on what Zenith Caste Exalted hope to accomplish and how they see their place in the world. The various anecdotes in this chapter serve to illustrate the world of **Exalted** and to show how members of the Zenith Caste hope to either fit within it or change it more to their liking. Guidelines are provided for some of the more potentially complicated concepts associated with playing and running the Hammers of Heaven.

Chapter Three: The World Awaiting Us gives the opinions of the five Zenith Caste Exalted on mortals, on other Exalted and on the wide range of supernatural beings they have encountered in their travels. The signature characters discuss, in their own words, the regions through which the five have traveled and the various political and supernatural forces that rule there.

Chapter Four: Voices Not Our Own shows the wide variety of opinions held by mortals and various powerful beings about the new Zenith Caste Exalted. Some seek to use them, while others see them as potential allies. Many fear the Zeniths, but all acknowledge that they are forces to be reckoned with. Players can also use the anecdotes in this chapter as a basis for possible opponents or allies for their characters.

Chapter Five: Dreams of the First Age offers information about the visions and memories of the First Age that occasionally come to all Solar Exalted and includes examples of the types of memories many Zenith Caste have about this lost era.

Chapter Six: Magic of the Zenith provides many new Charms for use by the Zenith Caste and other Solar Exalted. Additional Hearthstones and magical items, including magical weapons, also appear in this chapter. As the priests of righteousness, the Zenith Caste place particular importance on the four Virtues. Thus some of the Charms, Hearthstones and artifacts discussed in this chapter are intimately tied to these Traits.

Two appendices are also included with summaries of the narrating characters and five additional Zenith Caste Exalted characters. These templates might be used for inspiration for your own characters or as allies or opponents to be encountered.

Source Material

Passionate leaders are a staple of heroic tales from the earliest myths to modern film. Examples of righteous priests can be found in books, movies and television. Though good choices abound, players may find a few suggestions useful.

Movies and Television

The TV shows *Xena: Warrior Princess* and *Hercules: The Legendary Journeys* are both somewhat silly and lighthearted, but they can still be used as examples for Zenith Caste Exalted. In particular, comparing the portrayal of Gabrielle early in the series to her later portrayal provides a good example of a pre- and post-Exaltation righteous leader.

A much-overlooked Robert DeNiro film, *The Mission*, portrays a Catholic mission to the South American Indians in the early colonial era. Of particular interest is Robert DeNiro's character Mendoza, whose choice to fight, rather than pray, is illustrative of the Zenith Caste and its approach to life.

To get the feel for the action of the world of Exalted, there's nothing like Hong Kong cinema. The monk played by Chow Yun-Fat in *Crouching Tiger, Hidden Dragon* is an excellent example of a Zenith Caste priest, albeit one who doubts his mission. Other holy men from Hong Kong cinema and anime, such as Swordsman Yen from *Chinese Ghost Story* and Herai from *Doomed Megalopolis* also provide excellent examples of warrior-priests.

Finally, the priest in *William Shakespeare's Romeo + Juliet* excellently portrays a blazing light of righteousness in an unrighteous world.

Literature

Religion, history and myth are all wonderful sources for tales of inhumanly grand warriors and astoundingly skilled fighters.

The Old Testament of the Bible is filled with excellent examples of righteous priests, leaders and kings. Elijah, Samson and David offer different looks at potential Zenith concepts, and they are not the only ones. We urge you to look in particular to the books of Judges and Daniel for inspiration.

Other religious texts and historical documents provide additional examples of passionate crusaders. Muslim history supplies Umar and, at the dark end, el-Hajjaj. Joan of Arc and Rasputin both claimed to be gifted with divine visions, and each acted on those insights with conviction until their respective demises.

One excellent contemporary work on this topic is *The Grapes of Wrath*, which has two great characters on which to model concepts. Both the protagonist and the tent preacher gone honest are archetypal members of the Zenith Caste.

Modern storytellers have a new format in which to record the heroes of myth — comic books. *Rising Stars* features a number of potential Zenith Castes, including Joshua Kane and John Simon. The former is an example of a character willing to sacrifice anything for his ideals, while the later illustrates well the passionate leadership of the Zenith Caste.

Chapter One
Our Souls Through Our Eyes

The members of the Zenith Caste of the Solar Exalted are the first among equals, the keepers of righteousness and justice among their tribe. They are the Pillars of the Sun, the strong center around which the other castes gather. In the First Age, the Zeniths were the leaders of the Solar Deliberative and the Realm. Their wisdom and insight guided the Realm's bureaucracy and the armies with fairness and surety. Their voices fired the hearts and minds of the people and inspired them to greatness. Their deeds won the loyalty of their followers and guided them through their example.

But even the Pillars of the Sun were not perfect, and in time, their blazing light cast deep shadows. It was the curse laid upon them by the enemies of the gods as they were cast from the world. The adoration and devotion of the people turned the Zeniths away from honoring the Unconquered Sun and caused them to glorify themselves. They used the name of the Unconquered Sun to justify lies and pronouncements in their own interest. Corruption spread like a plague through the Realm, and the once-loyal followers of the Resplendent Suns turned against them. The Dragon-Blooded rose up and slew the Solar Exalted, and the Zeniths fell from their high pinnacle.

Now, in the Second Age of Man, the reborn Zenith Caste carries the word of the Unconquered Sun and the duty to lead as it did before, to guide humanity back to the path of righteousness. More than any other caste of Solar Exalted, the Zenith Caste is gifted with insight by the Unconquered Sun. The Golden Bulls hear his voice speaking to them at their Exaltation, and they know their duty under Heaven.

Members of the caste come from all peoples and all walks of life. Some led lives as priests, shamans, astrologers and philosophers before they were chosen. Others were common folk, soldiers, laborers, bureaucrats — even slaves and gladiators. What they share in common is a willingness to hear the voice of the Unconquered Sun and to act in the name of what is right, true and just, no matter what the consequences or who stands in their way. Their Exaltation burns away doubt and uncertainty in the purifying flame of the Unconquered Sun himself and gives the Zeniths a deep sense of purpose; it is up to them to save the world.

Here are the tales of some of the Hammers of Heaven, the Chosen of the Unconquered Sun.

Panther

I have been many things in my life: thief, slave, gladiator. I have stolen from the shops of merchants careless enough not to watch their wares. I have killed men for the pleasure of an audience, screaming for blood, and felt only joy that it was my opponent, and not I, to fall. I won my freedom from slavery through blood and murder.

I tell you this so you will understand that the purity of our caste, and of the Solar Exalted, is not the purity of a blank page awaiting ink or of a virgin awaiting that first caress. Ours is the purity of work and sweat that purges poison from the body. It is the purity of a white-hot fire that burns away clinker and slag, leaving only the finest metal to be forged and tempered until it is unbreakable. We were not chosen because we were pure, but because we could be *made* pure and whole by the divine power of the Unconquered Sun, as the world can be made pure and whole once again.

I was born in Nexus. I never knew my father. My mother told me only that he was a stranger. And there are many strangers in Nexus, especially along the Street of the Broken Lanterns, where I was a child. We were poor, terribly poor, and I often imagined as a boy that my father was a hero from some far-off land, perhaps even one of the Dragon-Blooded, and that, one day, he would return to us. He would take my mother and me away in a fine chariot, and we would sail aboard a white-winged ship to the fabled Blessed Isle itself and live in a palace. But that was not to be, and now, I would not wish to travel to the Blessed Isle with anything less than the mightiest army in the world at my back.

My mother died of a fever when I was still a boy. I had no money for medicines or charms to help her, not even enough to bury her. Her body was taken away in a rickety cart laden with other corpses to be shorn of their hair and then burnt at the public's expense. I lived alone on the streets, stealing what I could to survive, living among the rats and the vermin — human and otherwise.

Of course, I was caught. I was never an especially good thief. I was larger and stronger than most boys but not especially sly, and hunger twisted a knife in my belly that made me reckless. I was enslaved, since Nexus does not waste useful resources with executions. They called it indentured servitude, but it was slavery nevertheless. I was fortunate that my size and strength made me of interest to potential masters, even more that one saw me as a bodyguard or gladiator rather than a beast of burden. I was bought and trained to fight. I learned some swift — and painful — lessons in those first years, but I trained longer than most slaves were able to before their time came in the arena.

Yes, if you visited Nexus in the past few years, you might have heard of me. They called me the Panther, for my black skin and my grace in the pit — like a hunting cat, they said. I fought many matches, so many I lost count. I fought men and beasts, some armored, some not. I fought with sword and spear and khatar, mace and knife and cestus and, sometimes, with my bare hands. But most importantly, I won. I always won, and the crowd loved me for that. For a time, that was enough for me, the approval of the crowd and the chance to live in luxury and, perhaps, earn my freedom.

I made my owner a wealthy man, and I did win my freedom, a gift given for the blood I spilled. I remember the day when the door was opened to me and the world stood outside it. I looked out into the bright and dusty street for a long time before I turned my back on the world and walked back into the arena, the only world I knew. Fighting was all I understood. I didn't know there was anything else, but I learned soon enough.

Exaltation

The days after winning my freedom passed, one after the other. I fought and won great victories, and there was money, wine, drugs and many women who sought my company. But inside, I felt only emptiness, aching to be filled. I think that I would have died in the arena, except that I was trained too well. I fought without even thinking, and looking back, I can see how eager I was for the match that would prove to be my last.

One day, I lay in my apartment, like a cat lounging in the heat of the day — or, perhaps, a dead man awaiting burial — pondering my existence. That was when it came upon me, the glorious golden radiance that seemed to fill the room like water, the sense that something vast and powerful had entered into my room, had entered into me, headier than the finest wine. It was as if I'd awakened from a long slumber and my life up until then was only a half-remembered dream.

Everything seemed so bright, so clear. My senses were alive as if for the first time. The creak of the bed as I rose, the dry, dusty scent of the streets below, a few merchants shouting their wares, the laughter and catcalls from the Guild brothel down the street. All of these and more came to me, but they were nothing compared to the richness and warmth of the light and the sound of the voice that spoke to me.

"Go and see," it said. "Look at the face that has chosen you." I went toward the balcony where the light streamed in, walking like a drunken man, stepping out into the brightness, looking up at the glorious, golden mask of the sun, and the Unconquered Sun spoke to me.

"You who have no father," he said in a voice like the roar of the crowd, "I am your father now. You who shed blood and know not why, I give you a reason. In my anger, I turned my face from the world of men, but I shall do so no longer. Know you are among my chosen priests. Go, and make the world a righteous place as you know best. Take light into darkness, and know you act with my blessing."

The light seemed to flare around me, and I felt the searing kiss of the Unconquered Sun on my forehead. I felt power like I had never known course through my limbs, and I felt the dark void in my heart fill with newfound purpose. I stumbled back from the balcony as the light dimmed, but still, the walls of my apartment were turned golden by the light. Then, I realized that the light came from me, draped around me like a cloak, blazing from my head like a crown. I knew what I had become.

I'd heard tales of the Anathema like everyone else, and now, I knew that they were false, for I had seen the truth in the glory of the Unconquered Sun. I knew that my old life in Nexus was over — I gathered what things I would need and slipped away from the city that very night. For the first time in my life, I stood at the gates of the city leading out into the world. I recalled the day I won my freedom. This time, I did not turn away. I left the Nexus behind without a second thought and ventured out into the world that awaited me.

I walked eastward for all of that night and into the next day. For many days and nights I walked, without resting or sleeping, drinking little and eating less. My limbs were still flush with the power I could feel in every fiber of my being. My belly was filled, like the rest of me, with light and purpose. So, I continued to walk, past the small towns and hamlets I saw, careful to avoid them, uncertain of the welcome I would receive. I walked on and on until I reached the edge of a great wood.

The trees towered overhead, like nothing I had ever seen before, their dark canopy making deep shadows among their trunks. I could hear birds calling to each other from the branches and other animals scuttling through the underbrush. I knew about the spirits of the forest and the dangers they posed to lone travelers, yet, I stepped into the wood without fear, as if I walked the safest road in the Realm. The shadows cloaked me in coolness, but even at night, I could feel the Unconquered Sun above me, his golden light filtering through the leaves.

I walked further into the wood, going for many days and nights. I left the human places behind and listened to the songs and calls of the birds and beasts. It was as though they welcomed me into their home. I walked on as the trees grew taller and thicker, the light grew softer and the wood darkened around me. I walked until I reached a place where even the creatures' voices were still, and I came upon a path made of woven branches and fallen leaves, with trees stretching up all around me as far as the eye could see. The ground was their roots and the sky their leaves, a silent temple of stillness. There, I rested.

There in the silence, for the first and last time, I questioned why I was chosen. I never considered myself a wise man. I am not learned in lore, philosophy or letters. I had not the training of an Immaculate monk or even a tribal priest. My only skills were those of a gladiator. My only renown was for killing and surviving. Why was I chosen? What was I to do?

There beneath the shadows of the great trees, I meditated for the first time in my life. I drank sweet water that bubbled up between the trees roots, fasted and listened for the thunderous voice that had spoken to me. It did not come again, at least, not in the way I expected. I waited and listened but heard only silence. Then, in my heart, I heard the words of the Unconquered Sun again. "Go, and make the world a righteous place as you know best." I already knew what I had to do; the task was laid out before me. All that remained was for me to do it, and that was why I was chosen. I had felt the need to do something, to devote my life to a purpose. Now, my purpose was clear.

I left the silent temple of trees and walked out of the forest, back into the lands of men. There, I sought out what was wrong, and I have worked ever since to make the world a righteous place. All that remains to be seen is who else will take up the cause with me.

Ocean Pearl

My name is Ocean Pearl, captain of the *Scarlet Saber*. Ah, so you know *her* name if not mine, eh? Well, you'll be hearing mine soon enough. But you're wondering what became of Blackheart, the previous captain of the *Saber*, aren't you, the pirate no man could kill? Listen, and I'll tell you.

I knew that I was born to the sea from the time I was only a little girl. I spent all my free time at the shore, and I know there were people in my village who thought for sure I would fall victim to some siren that would call me out into the water and drag me down. But I learned to swim not long after I could walk, and I knew that the sea held no danger to me so long as I respected her. It's those who forget to respect the sea and her creatures who suffer their anger.

My parents wanted me to marry a local boy, settle down and raise a family. That's what's expected of women back home, but I wouldn't have any of it. The sea called, and I had to answer. I ran away from home with only the clothes on my back and some food and a few jade coins in a bag slung over my shoulder. I went to a small seaport town and sought commission on board a ship as a cabin girl. The ship didn't matter, so long as it would take me away from home and out to adventures on the sea.

Unfortunately, all I found was work as a serving girl in one of the taverns along the docks, but that was enough to allow me to meet Kajo, the captain of the merchant ship the *Misty Dawn*. Old Kajo took a liking to me and agreed to take me on. His ship was an old barnacle-encrusted tub with a crew that reeked of sweat and salt, a bilge that leaked and the worst food you can imagine, but to me, she was a floating palace, and I was happy for the opportunity. I had finally taken to the sea.

I sailed with Kajo for a few years and became a full member of his crew. I learned the ways of the sea and visited many of the islands of the Western Ocean, as well as ports along the southern coast of the Inland Sea. We had fought off pirates and even sea beasts, but never, before or since, have I encountered a man like Blackheart.

Blackheart, the Man With No Shadow — he was already a legend in these waters then, years ago. The sight of his ship struck terror into the hearts of sailors because they knew there was no escape from him. More importantly, they'd all heard the tales. Blackheart made a deal with the Deathlords, and no man could kill him. He cast no shadow even in the brightest day, some said because the Deathlords owned his soul, and he served his fell masters well. One day, as the *Misty Dawn* sailed under leaden skies, Blackheart's blood red and ebony flag appeared on the horizon.

We tried to flee, of course, but a merchant tub is no match for a swift catamaran. She caught us with ease, and Blackheart's crew clustered at the rails, weapons held high, shouting and laughing at our struggles to escape. We fought, and bravely, too, for all the good it did us. In the end, Kajo and most of the crew were killed, the rest of us taken prisoner, brought with our cargo and the corpses of our shipmates onto the pirate ship. I know now that we were to be given as prizes to Blackheart's master, the Deathlord Bodhisattva Anointed By Dark Water.

But when the captain came to inspect his catch, I caught his eye. While it is true that he had no heart and no shadow, Blackheart was a man in every other way. We struck a bargain. I would be his mistress, and my six surviving crewmates would go free. He could have taken me by force, but he wanted something else. He wanted me to give myself to him willingly, and so I did — I became the lover of the man with no heart.

Exaltation

At first, I was only Blackheart's mistress, but I quickly learned that gave me a measure of power on board his ship. More importantly, I knew there was something about me that Blackheart valued, something that made me more than just a bedmate or even a companion. I insisted on being a part of his crew, not just a trophy, and that seemed to please him. After all, I was as good a sailor as any on board the *Scarlet Saber*, and I aimed to prove it.

So I did. I won the admiration and respect of the roughnecks and outcasts who served on board that ship. It was hard. They hated me and saw me as an outsider. I showed them that I could sail and fight and drink as hard as any of them and won them over. I'm sure that my ability to sometimes mollify Blackheart's anger also earned me the gratitude and respect of the crew. I listened to their stories, many lies, but others true, about where they hailed from and how they came to this life.

We raided many ships. Blackheart was fearless, and his presence inspired his men. We took on any ship that came within our sight that held booty or men we could capture, since the Bodhisattva Anointed By Dark Water was always eager for new slaves. It was in those battles that I saw Blackheart's power at work and learned that the legends were true. He could not be killed, not by sword thrust or arrow, by steel or sorcery. His wounds closed before one's eyes. I once saw a woman on an enemy ship cut Blackheart's head from his shoulders. But the captain simply reached down, retrieved his fallen head and set it back on his neck like he'd lost his hat. Sights such as that rendered our crew fearless and made me despair. The man who murdered my friends and took my life was indeed invincible.

I suppose I could have escaped. I wasn't a prisoner on board the *Saber* — there were times when I even thought about silently lowering a launch into the water and slipping away into the night, letting the ship sail on without me and trying to find my way back to land alone. But I couldn't turn my back and run. My business with Blackheart wasn't finished, and I felt a kind of connection to the ship and its crew, if not its captain. His touch offended me more each night, and his smug confidence filled me with loathing for him. In time, I decided to attempt the impossible. I would lead a mutiny against Blackheart and overthrow him — or die trying.

I knew which members of the crew to talk to. I knew them better than they knew themselves, far better than Blackheart, who saw them only as instruments of his will. Some had been recruited much as I had, castoffs and prisoners accepted into the crew with nowhere else to go, their former lives destroyed by Blackheart. Others were merely discontent with the captain's iron-handed rule and feared his Deathlord master. All of them were certain that Blackheart couldn't be defeated, but I was able to persuade them that I would find a way, so long as they would follow me. I gathered the support of a small cadre I could trust. Then, I put my plan into action.

After a particularly successful raid, our hold was overflowing with prisoners and booty. Blackheart was flushed with success and looking to celebrate. I obliged him with many jugs of strong Haltan wine we'd captured, promising even greater pleasures that night. While the captain was in his cups, I praised his prowess as a warrior and asked him to tell me the tale of his invincibility.

Charmed and drunk on his own power, Blackheart told me how he swore to serve the Bodhisattva Anointed by Dark Water, how the Deathlord performed a sorcerous ritual wherein he gathered up the pirate's shadow like gauzy black cloth and cut open his chest to stuff it inside him. "Your shadow will be your shield," Bodhisattva said in his dead voice. "So long as it hides within you, death cannot claim you." Blackheart even showed me the jagged scar over his heart where the Deathlord had made the cut. Then, he collapsed against the pillows and fell asleep, his half-finished goblet of wine hitting the floor as he began to snore.

I quickly stole from his cabin, changed my clothes and retrieved my sword. Then, I went to Tanar, the man I trusted most among the crew and told him to spread the word: The time was now. We quickly gathered our forces and made our way to the hold, where we easily overpowered the guards before the stunned eyes of the prisoners. As my people moved to open their shackles, I raised my sword to them.

"Follow me," I said, "and you can be free of this place." As I spoke, I felt a fire kindle within my heart and a great weight lift from my chest. I breathed deeply of the salt air, as if for the first time, and a shining, golden light was all around me. A voice spoke to me with the sound of thunder above the waves.

"You who have suffered in bondage are now free. I am the Unconquered Sun, and I have seen your struggles. I hear the voices of all hearts that cry out for justice and righteousness in this world. Once, I turned my face away and made myself deaf to those cries, but no longer. As you raise your hand and your voice in the cause of righteousness, my daughter, I Exalt you above all others. Go, and bring your light into the darkness. Make right the world."

The voice faded, and I saw the faces of my crew and the prisoners, bathed in golden light, staring at me in slack-jawed awe. Light burned around me, and I could feel the mark of the Unconquered Sun shining from my brow. I raised my sword again. "Your deliverance is at hand! Who will seize it?" A shout went up from them as the freed prisoners grabbed weapons offered by my crew and I led the charge up onto the deck.

My sword was like a scythe in my hand. It clove through the first ranks of the men who opposed me, and my followers surged behind me. The rest of the crew was taken unawares, not expecting so furious an assault. They fell back before us, and I led the way, light shining around me like a beacon to guide us.

Our enemy rallied when Captain Blackheart burst from his cabin, sword in hand, his face twisted by rage. He spotted me amidst the melee and roared an oath that made the thunder crack and the ship pitch, then he charged at me. They cleared the deck around us as we clashed and sparks leapt from our swords.

"Harlot! Traitor!" Blackheart cried. "Is this how you repay my mercy? When I am finished with you, you will beg for death, and the Bodhisattva will make you into my undying plaything for all eternity!"

My answer was a flurry of blows his blade flashed to block. The last slipped through his defenses and left a narrow red gash along his chest, but Blackheart only laughed.

"Pitiful trull! I am Blackheart! The Man With No Shadow! I cannot be killed by any man!"

I took a step back, raising my sword between us. Then I glanced down at the deck behind Blackheart and smiled slowly. It dawned on Blackheart that the wound I'd given him was not healing, that both our men stood silent, watching us and looking at the same spot on the deck. Blackheart twisted his head and saw there, falling behind him, limned by the fiery light around me, was his cowardly shadow. Fear sparked in his eyes, and the breath caught in his throat.

"It… it cannot be!"

"It can," I said, "for mine is the power to drive out all shadows, even yours, a power greater than the Deathlords themselves! I am Ocean Pearl, Chosen of the Unconquered Sun, and your time of reckoning is at hand!" Then, I lunged forward, pressing the attack.

Blackheart was still a skilled warrior, but without the protection of his shadow, my sword nipped and nicked at him, and each cut that did not heal took some of his courage with it. He launched himself at me in a mighty attack, blade raised overhead, and I drove my sword deep into his chest, through the hollow heart that once held all the darkness of his spirit. Blackheart fell to the deck, dead at last.

So, you see, the *Saber* is my ship now. You may have heard of our raids against the ships of the Realm and the Guild. Those we capture may join us willingly or be freed. As for the treasures we've taken, this is but a sample. I'm sure it will help you to rebuild after what you have suffered.

Armattan

No, I wasn't born in Paragon, as you can see, and I'm grateful for that. Nor do I intend to die here, no matter what you might have heard. I have business in this city, and I've come a long way to get here. Once my business is concluded, I'll leave, but not before.

My name is Armattan. Some call me the Desert Lion. I come from Gem, at least originally, though, for the past few years, I haven't spent much time in the city. I was a caravan guard for some time, you see, traveling with the expeditions that left Gem to make their way into the southern deserts looking for the stones that make the Despot such a wealthy man.

It was difficult work, but it paid well enough that I enjoyed myself in the city in between jobs. Then, the money would run out, and I'd sign on to make the trip again. Sometimes, we encountered bandits or sand swimmers. I knew of caravans set upon by the Fair Folk, attacked by barbarians with scaled hides like snakes or even lost in the Wyld-touched places of the desert, where they wandered until starvation and madness overcame them, but I was fortunate enough never to have encountered such things myself.

A little less than a year ago, I ventured out with an expedition during the summer. It was the most miserable and dangerous time to travel the desert, but it was also when the prices of gems went up and firedust was easier to find among the dunes to the Far South. The pay was also better than usual, and I needed the money, so I went. We traveled at night, when the desert cooled, thankful for the warmth of the sand against the chill in the air. During the burning heat of the day, we sheltered in wagons and tents and slept as best we could. We made slow progress across the desert, with nothing but endless bleached sand stretching out before us as far as the eye could see.

The raiders came upon us while we traveled in the night. The only warning of the attack was when the man who was walking next to me cried out and fell to the ground with an arrow buried in his chest, his blood soaking into the thirsty sand. More arrows thudded into the wooden sides of wagons and into flesh as well. Then, the raiders came boiling up over the dunes, swathed in loose fitting robes and scarves that covered their heads and faces. We fought them as well as we could, but there were too many. One of them used a firewand, and a wagon exploded into flames, casting a bloody light over the battle.

I killed one of the raiders, then pulled my khatar from his body to turn and meet the rush of one of his brothers. But I was too slow, and his sword took me in my left side. I felt the blade scrape against my ribs and hot wetness pour down my side. I slashed the man with my khatar, tearing his robe and cutting his sword-arm. He cursed, and his knee met my stomach, sending the air rushing out of my lungs. As I stumbled back, he transferred his sword to his other hand, and I saw, on the palm of his right hand, a sign like an open, staring, eye tattooed there in red, glowing faintly. Then the pommel of his sword met my skull with a crack, and I pitched forward into the dust, blackness claiming me.

Exaltation

I awoke to the screeching and squawking of the carrion birds gathered to feast and felt the burning heat of the sun on my back. I lifted my head and winced from the pain of the wound in my side, then I rolled over and spit the sand and grit from my mouth, my tongue swollen and dry as leather. All around me lay the bodies of my companions and the ruins of our wagons. The wagon set afire was a smoldering heap, and the sand was splashed with dark stains of blood, some of it my own. Of our camels, there was no sign. The bandits took everything of value and left the rest to the scavengers.

For a moment, I profoundly regretted waking at all. Better, I thought, to have died peacefully in my sleep than to perish of hunger and thirst alone in the desert, only to rise again, cursed to haunt the site of my murder with the ghosts of my unburied fellows. It would take nearly a week to reach Gem, alone and on foot, and I had nothing to aid me in my journey. I tried to catch one of the desert birds, but they took wing too quickly, and I was too slow. They cawed and squawked as if mocking me. Despair overwhelmed me, and I fell to my knees in the sand. Raising my fist to Heaven, I swore vengeance against our attackers, calling justice to fall upon them. At that moment, I was Exalted.

The burning sun above spoke to me in words like the roar and hiss of a sandstorm. "You who have fallen victim to the greed and cruelty of other men, I offer you succor and place the power to seek justice in your hands. Once, I blinded myself to injustice and wrongdoing, but no more. Rise, my son, and let your thirst be quenched by righteousness. Let your hunger be satisfied by justice. Return to the world of men, and take my message with you."

Visions filled my mind, of battles and heroes, of betrayal and grave injustice. I fought at the side of my fellows, my blade wet with blood, but it was not the fight against the bandits. It was a great and terrible battle. I saw my wife cut down before my eyes, and my heart swelled with the need for vengeance. Then, the vision faded. The dark-haired woman was not my wife, not in this life, but the burning need to right the wrongs I had seen still filled me.

I swayed to my feet and raised my arms to the Unconquered Sun, feeling his light fill me, then pour from me like a fountain. The bodies of the fallen all around me burst into flame as the light touched them, the smoke carrying their spirits toward Heaven as the fire cleansed the remains of the bandits' bloody work, leaving only fine gray ash that mixed with the sand.

Rather than turning back the way we came, toward Gem, I turned toward where the bandits had fled and began walking, my stride becoming surer with each step I took. The signs of the bandits' passing were as clear to me as the blazing sun overhead. It was as if a veil had been lifted; my senses were alive as never before. Each disturbance of the sand, every drop of blood, even the scents carried to me by the wind, spoke volumes. As I traveled, the pain from my wound troubled me less and less, and the burning heat of the sun on my back became a gentle, soothing warmth.

As I walked, tireless and resolute, more visions came to mind, faded ghosts of memory flitting through my head. I saw bright cities of shining marble, with columns of jade and domes of crystal and gold. I lounged with my back against the trunk of an orange tree, breathing in the heady scent of the blossoms, opening my eyes to see the smile of a pair of lips as red as blood in a pale face. I fled burnt and in terror through darkened streets as the thunder of booted feet closed in behind me. I slipped in a pile of garbage and rolled to a stop in an alley, just as dark figures gathered around me and a woman in jade armor stepped in front of them, a naked blade in her hands.

When night came, I found shelter in the lee of a rocky outcropping and tended my wound. My fingers held new wisdom, and the bandage I wrapped around my chest soothed the ache and allowed me to rest. More dreams came to me in the night, but foremost was the image of the bandit I fought and the red eye glowering from his palm before he struck the final blow. It was still dark when I woke, but I felt filled with energy and purpose. I set off again at once, following the trail, even in the dark of night.

I had not been walking long when I felt a presence close at hand. I reached for the khatar sheathed at my side and had just laid my hand upon it when a desert lion leapt from behind another outcropping and roared. I spun toward the beast, both of us tensed to pounce, but then, I let go of the hilt of my weapon and approached the lion slowly with my hands open. I felt a sense of recognition, of kinship, with this proud beast. The lion was confused by my bold approach and hesitated for a moment.

"I mean you no harm," I said in a soothing tone. "I am a hunter, like you, but you are not my prey, nor am I yours." My eyes locked with the golden eyes of the cat, and an understanding passed between us. Our meeting was destined, ordained by the Unconquered Sun.

"I am Armattan," I said, going down on one knee, now only an arm's length away. The great cat padded forward and butted her head against my chest, a deep purr thrumming through her. "What is your name?" I asked, and she looked up at me. I looked into her eyes. "Sirah," I said. "Your name is Sirah." She emitted a rumble of pleasure. Sirah has been my companion in the hunt since then, the first of many, I hope.

Fire Orchid

"Destiny shows in the blood," they say in the Realm. I always hated that saying, but perhaps there is some truth to it after all. I never thought it applied to me because it meant that my destiny was to be a humble one, and that would never do for a scion of the Karal gens, especially not the first-born child of the great General Linwei. My mother named me Fire Orchid because she said I was as beautiful as a blossom but also had a fire burning within me.

I knew even as a child that my mother was a great woman, respected throughout Lookshy, and none loved and respected her more than I did. When my younger brothers were born, I took to heart my mother's advice, to be a good example for them, a responsible older sister.

How bitter, then, to discover as I approached womanhood that I was not among the Chosen, that my spirit was not pure enough to carry the family's power within it. At first, my parents believed I was a late bloomer, that my gifts would come in time. But as the months and years passed, it became clear that the fire my mother saw in me was not the fire she wielded, that made her enemies tremble. It was even whispered that it was because my father was clubfooted that I did not Exalt. How can I describe the sense of relief I felt from my parents when my brothers both proved to be among the Exalted. My mother turned her attentions to them, her true heirs, as her hopes for me wilted and died.

Of course, it would not do for the daughter of such a distinguished officer to bear such disgrace with anything less than perfect dignity. I kept my head held high in public and cried myself to sleep at night. My mother arranged a commission for me in the Seventh Legion, both as an obligation to the daughter who was once the apple of her eye and, I imagine, as a means of making something of me in this life. I began as a low-ranking officer, and many of my superiors were Dragon-Blooded — I was determined to prove myself worthy of my mother's trust, to show that I could be the child she wanted.

And prove myself I did. For nearly 40 years, I served with the field forces. My brothers served as well and rose to positions of influence, which they hold still, since their careers would be longer than I could measure with my whole life. I campaigned on the worst battlefields of the Threshold. I struggled through mud and mire, waded through blood, charged through fire, all the while upholding the colors of Lookshy and the legion faithfully.

I won accolades and medals, but I gained something even more precious to me, the respect of my troops and of the officers I served with. I did not command the powers of fire, but I was still my mother's daughter. I had a knack for military matters and, more importantly, for leadership. When I was placed in command of my own scale, my troops were willing to follow me to the ends of Creation, if need be.

In time, I rose to command an entire wing, as far as a mere mortal could be expected to rise. I was proud of my service to the legion and of the loyalty of my troops. But I tired of the blood and the battles, of the struggles and of growing old while my brothers remained as youthful as ever. I grew wary of the litanies of the Immaculates, whose only hope for me was that I might achieve the "spiritual perfection" of my brothers in my next life, if I proved worthy.

Meanwhile, my brothers gathered glories and climbed the legion's chain of command. While they still had the vigor of young men, I had grown old. I'd chosen not to marry, partly because of my career and partly because I didn't want the kind of marriages I was offered — men eager to marry the unExalted daughter of such a prominent general, knowing my far more readily available blood carried the seed of Exaltation that could make their sons and daughters great. Then, Thorns fell and the Scarlet Empress disappeared, and it became clear that the great houses would struggle for control of the Realm. It was only a matter of time before the conflicts reached Lookshy, and I was too old for the wars that were blowing in the wind.

So, I retired. I took the wealth I'd earned over the years and bought a villa in the Hundred Kingdoms, near a small village called Rana, where I planned to spend my remaining years raising grapes and figs, away from all of the conflicts. But it was not to be.

Exaltation

Oh, it was peaceful enough, for a few short years. Word of happenings in Lookshy and the Realm rarely reached my ears, though I heard some news from my servants or whenever I went into the village myself. There were concerns over the Arczechk tribes, but we saw no trouble from them for the first few years that I lived near Rana. The harvests were good, and I forgot, for a time, the life I'd left behind.

But then, one day, an outcry came from the village. I was weeding in the garden when Masi, a boy who oftentimes carried parcels to me, came running up my path as if the hosts of the Wyld were at his heels. He had only time to cry out "Mistress!" before a shining silver arrow took him in his leg and he pitched forward into the dust of the road.

The thunder of hooves and the jangling of golden and silver bells sounded as a troupe of riders approached and fear clutched my heart in an icy grip. Neither riders nor steeds were of earthly origin. They were pale and delicate and resplendent in armor of gold and silver, copper and spun crystal, swathed in brightly colored silks. The lead rider lowered his ivory bow and spurred his horse forward toward the wounded boy who lay in the path.

I acted without thought, seizing the hoe that stood close at hand and rushing to Masi's side. He moaned and tried to move, as I stood astride him and the horseman reined in his mount. He was the most beautiful creature I had ever seen, flesh as pale as marble, hair and eyes like molten silver. His mouth twisted in a cruel smile, and I imagined the image before him: an old woman in dirt-stained clothes, holding him at bay with a farm hoe. I took note of the smoke beginning to rise in the distance.

He laughed, a sound like a waterfall, as he looked down at me. "Who are you to interfere with my sport?"

I stood my ground although my guts were turning to water within me. "I am Karal Fire Orchid, noble visitor, and this is my home."

He glanced up at the villa before turning his silvery gaze back to me. "Is it? My apologies then, for not introducing myself more properly." He made a mocking bow from his saddle. "I am Hayashi, a noble of the people beyond the edge of Creation, and you are standing between me and my prey, old woman."

"This lad is no prey of yours."

"Ah, but he is, so you may either step aside or..." the Fair Folk's threat was cut off as I stepped forward and swung the hoe. Its iron blade struck Hayashi's arm with a sizzling sound, and he screamed in pain. In that inhuman cry, I heard my own death, for I knew that I could not stand against one of the Fair Folk, much less Hayashi and his troupe.

Still, I made a good fight of it. My few servants wisely fled while the Fair Folk took their sport with me. I left the faerie with a few marks to remember me by, but it wasn't long before my makeshift weapon was torn from my hands and a blow to my head sent me reeling. Hayashi cursed in an alien tongue as his hunters dragged Masi and me to my house. They hurled us roughly to the floor and turned to leave. I wildly hoped they had grown bored with us, but no. The door slammed shut and there was a whooshing sound. Suddenly, the whole of the house was ablaze, and I heard the silvery laughter of the Fair Folk as they watched it burn.

Then, a voice called out to me. At first, I thought it was Masi, but he had fainted from the pain of his wound. This voice was like the roar of the fire that surrounded us. I raised my aching head to see bright sunlight streaming through the window. The smoke stung my eyes and made the light seem to sparkle.

"Daughter of Fire," the voice spoke to me. "You have nurtured the spark within you. Now I will fan it into a flame." I felt my heart soar, and the heat of the flames around me was only a shadow compared to the fire I felt burning within me. "Once, I turned my face from the world, but no longer. You are among my

Chosen, and you will lead the world back into righteousness. Into your hands, I deliver the fate of all Creation. Strike down the unrighteous with your fury, and guide others with your wisdom."

I felt a strength I'd never known before course through my tired limbs, and I stood straight and tall. Masi groaned, his eyes opening and going wide as he saw me standing over him. He opened his mouth to say something but began to cough from the smoke gathering around us. He reached out for me, and I held his hand.

"Don't be afraid," I told him.

My thoughts went to the old armor and weapons I kept in a trunk as a remembrance. The light flared around me, and in an instant, I was armored and girded for battle. I bent down and scooped Masi up in my arms, then leapt through the window, scattering shards of glass and landing in a crouch outside. Even the Fair Folk were startled by my sudden appearance, dressed in my armor of enameled steel, as red as blood. I lowered Masi gently to the ground beside me and drew my blade, the glorious white-gold light burning around me, brighter than the flames behind me.

"Come on, then," I said, "and take your sport with me now, if you dare."

Two of the Fair Folk rushed forward, and I met their charge with my blade. I spun and blocked, then I struck. My sword pierced gossamer mail and silken cloth alike, and blood the color and odor of dark wine stained my foe's pale flesh. I whirled, blocked and struck again, rewarded with a cry of pain. Our battle was a dance whose steps I knew well, and I could not help but laugh aloud at the confusion and even fear I saw among Hayashi's small band.

"Back!" I shouted to them. "Back, for I am the Chosen of the Unconquered Sun! Run, rabbits, or feel my anger!"

The Fair Folk turned almost as one and fled, but Hayashi paused and regarded me, his silver eyes seething. Then, he galloped after his fellows, but I knew it would not be the last time that I saw him.

Wind

"The soul is not Exalted through birth, but through the journey of life, of which each birth is but a single step." So said Mela, Immaculate of Air, Petitioner of Clouds Accordant to the Call of Battle, in the Immaculate Texts. There is still wisdom in those words, although they do not hold the same meaning they once held for me. Once, I thought the divine Mela's meaning was that the journey of our lives along the road of enlightenment brings us one day to the glory of the Dragon-Blooded. This birth was not an accident, but a sign to us that a purified soul had incarnated into the world along the final steps of its journey. Yet, now, I see that no soul is Exalted by birth, not even the Dragon-Blooded, but, instead, by its deeds in this life. There is much for me to learn, and to teach, about the truth.

I am Wind, named for the strong gusts that blew on the day of my birth, and I was often told that my feet would carry me wherever the wind blows across the face of Creation. Certainly, I was always seized with a desire to travel and to see the world as a child. As the youngest son of four, I had little hopes of inheriting much from my family, so I was expected to make my way in the world on my own.

My parents were pleased when I chose to apply to the order and become a monk. I'd always felt that my life was a journey toward an end that I could not yet see, so the teachings of the Immaculate Order spoke to me. I realized that the journey was that of my soul and that becoming a monk would be another step toward achieving enlightenment, if not in this life, then in the next.

Of course, as a mere human, I could not rise to the heights of the Dragon-Blooded, but I was content to serve and to learn from more enlightened souls, as the human disciples of Mela learned from her how to channel their Essence and gained greater understanding. I had little doubt which of the Immaculate Dragons I would devote myself to, even before I entered the temple.

Life as a novice was hard, but I threw myself into my duties with all my heart and earned the praise of my teachers. There were chores to be done, exercises and training drills, meditations, sutras to recite and studies of the Immaculate Texts and other holy books. I was especially taken with the stories of those monks who traveled the world in search of new Immaculate Texts and artifacts of the First Age, to tell us more about our divine patrons and help guide us to emulate them and follow in their footsteps to enlightenment. I wanted to travel the world as part of that search.

I also made friends among my new brothers and sisters. The foremost were Kirin, closer to me than any of my brothers by blood, and Gentle Song. Kirin was a Dragon-Blood from the House of V'neef, and I was honored to have him choose me as a friend. But Gentle Song's company was the most precious to me. She was the most gracious and beautiful woman I had ever known, and I was in awe of her keen mind and knowledge of the ancient texts. Kirin helped to teach me to fight, although I was never any match for him, while Gentle Song helped me to understand the Immaculate Philosophy. The three of us became inseparable companions and remained so even after we took our vows.

Exaltation

My duties with the order led me to places I would never have imagined. How I long for those innocent days of exploration and friendship! I traveled with my fellow monks across the face of Creation in search of the lost lore and treasures of the First Age. Our travels brought us from the islands of the Western Ocean to the forests of the East, from the deserts of the South to the most desolate glaciers of the North. It is there that my journey ended and a new one began.

A small party from our order traveled to the city of Gethamane. Kirin and Gentle Song were a part of it, along with old Soolian and Autumn Frost. The city stood high in the mountains of the Far North, nestled against the side of a peak as if it were watching for something — or trying to hide from something, perhaps. It was an ancient place, a city of the First Age, although now inhabited by folk who fled the Great Contagion and the advance of the Fair Folk long ago. Standing in its vast halls, I could feel a strange sense of the familiar, like a place seen once in a dream and forgotten, until something reminds you of it.

The inhabitants knew well enough to leave us be, particularly with Kirin along. A glance at the greenish cast to his skin, much less the hammer of white jade he wore at his belt, was enough to convince them that we were well guarded. I felt there was something waiting for us in Gethamane and had high hopes of uncovering ancient artifacts or perhaps even a new Immaculate Text, despite the fact that much of the city had been picked over by scavengers already. But there were many parts of Gethamane that lay unexplored, including the rat's maze of tunnels running beneath the city.

Along with my feelings of anticipation and familiarity, I had a sense of being watched from the moment we came within sight of the city. That first night, as we prepared for sleep, I told Kirin about it, and he said that I was probably just nervous but that he would keep close watch. As I drifted off to sleep, I felt a presence close at hand. I bolted up from my sleeping mat and looked around the room but saw nothing but moonlight shining through the small window.

I drifted off to sleep again, but I was awoken by the terrible sound of a man screaming. I leapt from my sleeping mat and grabbed my sword, running for the door. Many other people, including the members of my own party, rushed out to see what was happening. Gentle Song looked into the narrow alley beside the inn and shrieked. There lay the lower half of a man's body, with much blood about but no sign of what became of his upper half.

I wanted to comfort Gentle Song and reassure her, but I caught sight of something moving out of the corner of my eye, up along the rooftops. I should have told Kirin or the others about it, but just then, it dipped behind a roof. I circled around the inn in time to see the shadowy figure leap from one roof to the next. Without any thought of what it might be, I followed it. I blundered into a blind alley and came up short in front of a blank wall. Then, I heard a whisper of movement behind me. I spun, my sword at the ready, and stopped.

It was a man, a youth, in fact, since he looked younger than me. He was thin and wiry, dressed all in black, with a cloak of black feathers that made it seem as if there were great wings on his back. His exposed skin was pale, covered with intricate tattoos of blue. His eyes were of the same deep color, his hair as black as the feathers of his cloak and falling wild about his shoulders. He cocked his head like a bird, looking at me curiously. On his forehead gleamed a silver circle.

I gasped, loud in the silence of the alley as I realized what he was. I knew that I should fear being torn apart like the poor wretch by the inn, yet strangely I didn't feel afraid. Instead, I felt intensely curious about this myth given form before me. Moreover, it was as if I knew him somehow and that he knew me. My sword dipped toward the ground, and I took a step forward, reaching for him without thinking.

"Who...," I began, and suddenly, there was a flurry of motion, a blur of dark feathers, and he vanished.

"No, wait!" I cried, but he was gone. A moment later, Kirin rushed into the alley, having followed me.

"Wind, are you all right? What happened?"

"I... I thought I saw something," I replied, looking up toward the rooftops. "But, whatever it was, it's gone now."

"You should be more careful," my friend said, putting a hand on my shoulder. "You're a good fighter, Wind, but no match for one of the Fair Folk or something from the Wyld." If only Kirin knew how right he was. I nodded in agreement, and we made our way back to the inn. Soolian was firm that the unpleasantness would not deter us from our mission. We had not traveled all the way the Gethamane to turn back now. I didn't sleep much for the rest of the night, my mind troubled by images of the lithe, pale man in the feathered cloak. Why would one of the Anathema flee from a mere mortal? Had he sensed Kirin's approach? And why did he seem so familiar to me?

Each of the next three nights, there was another death, as gruesome as the first. The heathen priests of the city's three temples began chanting and playing strange music day and night. The people in the city burned incense and surrounded their doors and windows with charms of paper, string and beads, scattering salt and seeds across every threshold. Everyone stayed inside and watched one another warily. Gentle Song even said that there was some talk that we might have brought some curse upon them, and Kirin warned us against going off alone.

Our search was proving fruitless, and my sleep was troubled by strange dreams. On the fifth night of our stay in Gethamane, I awoke from another dream with a start to find the Anathema from the alley crouched at the foot of my sleeping mat, silently watching me. I started to reach for my sword, but his hand flashed out and caught mine in a grip like steel, his eyes locked on mine. I struggled but to no avail. I wanted to cry out, but my voice was paralyzed, my throat dry. I could only manage a hoarse whisper.

"Have you come to kill me, too?" I asked. The pale stranger cocked his head, and I wondered for a moment if he even understood me. Then he spoke in a soft voice that was the most beautiful I had ever heard.

"I haven't killed anyone here... yet," he said. "I am Raiton. I came... to find you. Visions in the ice and clouds guided me to you. It has been a very long time." He reached out and brushed a slim hand against my cheek, and his touch was cool and strangely comforting. A tear trembled at the corner of his eye for a moment before spilling down his face, glistening in the pale moonlight slanting through the shutters. I felt my heart pounding, my breath quickening from his touch, his closeness. I was dizzy, and my skin felt flushed. I felt his grip on my wrist loosen.

Then, a high-pitched scream shattered the silence between us, coming from very close at hand.

"Gentle Song!" I cried, scrambling for my sword. My visitor leapt into a crouch, like a startled beast, and watched me with wild eyes. As I scooped up my sword, I gave no thought to the door. Instead, I struck the thin wall of withes and plaster between our rooms, shattering it with a single blow.

In the room beyond was Gentle Song, held in the grip of a monstrosity of flowing limbs, eyes and mouths — a horror painful to look upon. It filled me with a deep sense of loathing as white and golden light flared all around me, filling the room. The creature shrank away from my radiance. I struck at it with my sword, and black blood poured from the wound as a high-pitched wailing filled the air. It returned my blow with a force that sent me staggering.

Suddenly, a blur of blackness flashed past me, and Raiton grappled with the beast, his hands twisting into talons like those of a bird of prey. A moment later, the door burst in and Kirin leapt into the room, wielding his white-jade hammer, with sparks flashing all around it. The three of us fell upon the creature, flanking it, striking with sword and claw and hammer while the inn shook so that I thought it might collapse before the battle was done. The monster flailed at us with its loathsome limbs, but no matter which way it turned, another one of us attacked it. It began to back away, and we pressed the attack. A single eye, as large as my fist, turned up to squint at me. I drove my sword into it to the hilt. The creature shrieked its last, then it shuddered and began melting into a foul-smelling pool that spread across the floor.

In the silence that followed, a thunderous voice seemed to fill the room along with a blinding light, and I realized that the strange chanting of the temple priests had stopped.

"In the light, the truth will be revealed to you, my son," the voice said to me. "Bring the light of truth to others, and show them the glory I have given you. Heal the wounds that have been inflicted upon the world, and lead the people back to righteousness. That is the task I lay before you, my chosen priest, for I am the Unconquered Sun, your god."

The light faded, and I saw Kirin and Gentle Song staring at me in shock, eyes and mouths wide. I opened my mouth, ready to explain, to tell them there was nothing to fear, but the words failed me. I saw Raiton push open the window and crouch there, looking back at me.

"Come with me," he said, "and quickly." I glanced back at the looks of shock and horror on the faces of my closest friends, then at the wild and feral face of a man I hardly knew, who was Anathema. But then, what was I?

Raiton slipped out into the night, and I followed close behind him.

Chapter Two
Obligations of the Caste

Great is the power of the Zenith Caste, and equally great is its responsibility, for the Zeniths are the guiding light of the Solar Exalted. Once, they were the rulers of the world, chosen by the Unconquered Sun and granted the wisdom and the power to judge the people and guide them toward righteousness. The Zeniths were the priest-kings of the Old Realm, who glorified the Unconquered Sun and ruled the world with a firm but even hand, coordinating the efforts of their brothers and sisters among the Exalted.

After the Dragon-Blooded rose up and murdered the Solar Exalted, the Zeniths became known as the Blasphemous, the most corrupt and evil of the Anathema. Tales spread of how they forced the people to worship their evil gods, how they practiced bloody sacrifices and profane rites, before the coming of the Immaculate Dragons.

Now, the reborn Zeniths are rediscovering their ancient roles. Fortunately, they have the guidance of the Unconquered Sun to help them, so they, in turn, can help guide other Solar Exalted. There is much work for the Pillars of the Sun to accomplish, yet not all of these most fervent and dedicated of the Exalted agree on the best way to achieve their goals. While other Solar Exalted may deny their divine destiny, at least for a time, the Resplendent Suns cannot put aside their responsibilities so easily. The Unconquered Sun has called, and they have answered, and there is much work to be done in the world.

The Goals of the Zenith Caste

The foremost goal of the Zenith Caste is to restore the world to the path of righteousness. It is a difficult task indeed, since there is so much unrest and corruption today in Creation. Some Resplendent Suns are daunted by the vastness of the duty laid out before them, but in times of despair, they look to the unfailing light of the Unconquered Sun and the light that burns within each of them for guidance. They know what is right; they need only have the courage to act and the eloquence to show others the way.

The Pillars of the Sun promote righteousness through example. They know it is deeds and not words that ultimately sway the hearts and minds of men, so they perform deeds that root out and punish the wicked and support righteousness in the world. These wandering priests of the Unconquered Sun fight bandits, marauding barbarians, Fair Folk, hostile spirits and other forces of oppression and destruction. In their wake, the Zeniths leave a populace that has seen one more example of the power and righteousness of the Solar Exalted, people who begin to doubt the Dragon-Blooded stories of Anathema a bit more.

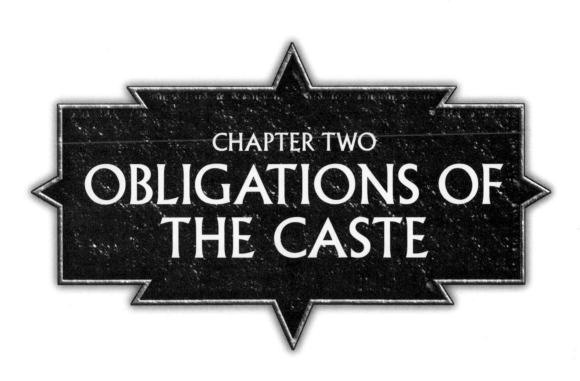

To achieve their goals, many of the Golden Bulls believe they must overthrow the Dynasty of the Dragon-Blooded and reclaim their rightful place as rulers of the Realm. These Zeniths wish to take the Realm's reins not out of a thirst for power, but to keep power from the hands of those who have abused it, to use that power to right the wrongs of the world. Of course, the Zeniths know that directly challenging the host of the Dragon-Blooded is too great a task even for them, at least for now, but they see the weakening of the Realm as an opportunity to tear it down and build anew on the foundations of old.

The Zeniths are agents of justice in the world. And not the justice of the Realm and its magistrates, so often subject to bribery and the whims of politics. No, the Hammers of Heaven are swift, sure, uncompromising justice that seeks out and punishes the wicked as a warning to those who might follow their example. When the head of a bandit chieftain is presented to his followers, they think twice about continuing to trouble that region. When the crimes of a corrupt noble are exposed, those who rule are forced to deal with them. When the people are truly united, no corrupt government can stand.

The Pillars of Heaven are leaders, born to guide others to the right path and to inspire mortal and Exalted alike with the courage and determination to face any threat, no matter how terrible. In the Threshold, the Golden Bulls find people in dire need of their leadership, abandoned by the legions of the Realm, ruled by weak or despotic leaders, threatened by barbarians, Fair Folk, hungry ghosts and monsters from the Wyld. The Zeniths show these people not only the power of the Exalted, but also the power even mortals hold when they work together as one.

And, finally, the Solar Thunder is the voice of the Unconquered Sun. The Zeniths carry with them the truth they each learned upon their Exaltation, a truth that must be spread to everyone. They know that the Unconquered Sun turned his face from the world once but that he has returned. They know the tales told of the Anathema are half-truths, that the litanies and sutras of the Immaculate Order are lies. They know that the Incarna are real and powerful. It is the Zeniths duty to bring light into the darkness of ignorance and deception, to show people the truth and the shining dream of a greater world that awaits them, if only they have the courage to follow where the Zenith Caste leads.

Panther on Righteous Action

It is not enough just to *know* what is right. You have to *act* on your knowledge, or it becomes meaningless. So many in this world see wrongs being done and do nothing out of fear: fear of punishment, fear of losing what they have, fear of death. The fire of the Unconquered Sun burns away fear. Even before I was chosen, the light of the sun on my back in the arena took away my fear. I knew that I would die, it was just a matter of when, and I chose to fight with all of my strength to survive for another day. When you accept your death, there is nothing more to fear.

I was chosen to see the wrongs in this world and to act to correct them. If we Zenith are to be beacons of righteousness to the world, then it must be through our actions, not our words. The Immaculate monks speak of righteousness and enlightenment, while children starve and are enslaved in the streets of Nexus. The Scarlet Houses loudly proclaim that they are each the best suited to lead the Realm to greatness, while plotting and scheming against each other in the shadows. It takes nothing to speak of righteousness, but it requires courage to risk yourself in its cause.

When I first returned to the world of men from the depths of the forest, I came upon a village. Barbarians from the edge of the world had invaded it. They were burning and sacking the place, slaughtering all who stood in their way and even many who did not. Once, the legions of the Realm might have come to push back the barbarians and protect the villagers, but the legions do not come so far into the Threshold any more, now that their Empress is gone. So, who is there to protect the people? What army sees the rape and slaughter and takes up arms against it? In the Threshold, everyone minds their own business, unless they're the ones threatened. Then, they cry out for aid and mercy and find that everyone ignores them, just like they ignored the cries of others. But we Zeniths do not ignore the cries for justice, for righteousness — we cannot.

I walked down from the hills into that village, where the barbarians enjoyed their sport. They wore only the furs of strange beasts, and their bodies were covered with paint and blood. It was no longer a battle, it was a slaughter, and it reminded me of fights in the arena rigged for the amusement of the crowd, where one of the contestants was drugged or unskilled and had no chance. The air was full of the smell of fire and blood, and bodies were scattered everywhere. Nearby, I saw a barbarian raise his stone axe to smash the skull of a woman he'd just violated.

I let my Essence flare around me like a corona. "Stop!" I shouted, my voice echoing like thunder above the din, and dozens of eyes turned toward me. They saw the majesty of the Unconquered Sun burning around me, and they hesitated. That was when I leapt at the barbarian closest to me and struck him with my armored gauntlet. He fell like a sapling, his axe tumbling to the ground, and the sound of his skull cracking broke the spell over the rest of his band. With a roar of battle cries, they charged toward me, and I laughed at them in defiance.

The fallen axe, I picked up and used to strike off the heads of the first two to reach me. Its stone blade shattered after striking down a third, so I discarded the twisted haft onto his corpse. With one gauntleted hand, I smashed through the hafts of spears they thrust at me, and I drew my own blade with the other. Their attacks were those of the bloodthirsty and the desperate that I'd seen in the arena so many times. They fought without discipline or strategy, sometimes striking each other in their rush to reach me. My blade wove a net of steel around me, and the barbarians that approached paid the price with their lives. My anima burned fiercely, my Caste Mark shining like the sun itself.

The barbarians charged and fell under my scything blade, their blood staining the ground red. Clashing weapons, war cries and screams of pain filled the air with the music of battle, while limbs and heads and bodies piled around me.

As I fought, I could feel the eyes of the villagers on me as well, like the crowd watching my performance from the stands, waiting with bated breath to see if I would live or die. So I played to them, laughing at the attacks of the barbarians, mocking them, calling them weak and cowardly. I rebuked their attack on the village and incited its people to strike back against their attackers. I showed them that their enemy was not invincible, but neither was I. In my feints and my counterattacks, I made it clear that I could not hold out forever, although I had no fear of the enemy I fought.

As I fended away an axe blow with one hand and drove my blade through a foe with the other, I became aware of sounds at the edge of the battle, of the building roar of the crowd. The villagers picked up farm implements, skinning knives, hunting bows and the fallen weapons of their enemies and charged the barbarians. The invaders were so focused on me that the attack took them completely by surprise, as their former victims fell upon them like a crashing wave and took vengeance for the pain the barbarians had inflicted.

I redoubled the fury of my attacks, calling out to the people to drive the barbarians from their village, and the will of the raiders broke. The barbarians fled toward the East, leaving their dead and their spoils behind. Calling on the power of the Unconquered Sun, I brought fire down upon the bodies of the dead, cleansing the fields and the square of the village. No hungry ghosts or nemissaries would trouble the villagers.

Then, I spoke to the people of that village, much as I am speaking to you now, and I will tell you what I told them. The Solar Exalted have returned to the world. We did not leave you of our own free will, and now that the Unconquered Sun has brought his blessings back to Creation, we have returned. I am one of his Chosen, sent to guide you back to the path of righteousness. I ask for neither jade nor other tribute from you. Instead, I ask that you live an upright life and help guide others to do the same. As I have seen here and in many other places, when people are united in the cause of righteousness, nothing can stand against them.

"But the Realm is too mighty!" you say. "The barbarians cannot be overcome!" I have heard these and a hundred other claims, so I ask you, what is the Realm without subjects to rule? If the world rises up against them, then who will the Dragon-Blooded command? Those villagers who hid from the barbarians' raid were slain just the same as those who fought back. Of what use is a life lived in fear? Better to stand up for righteousness and be struck down than to cower in a living death for all of your days. We are sent by the Unconquered Sun to guide and help you, but you must have courage, or else, all our might means nothing. Devote yourselves to righteousness and honor the gods, and we will make the world anew.

A fire begins with a small spark, and a great tree grows from a small seed. So it will be with the righteousness of the world. I know this. When I was first Exalted, I believed that it would be a simple matter to show everyone the way, but the misdeeds of centuries cannot be undone in a year, or in ten, or even in a lifetime. The struggle to restore the balance of our world will take a long time, and even when we are successful, the battle will not be over. There will always be those who will abuse their power, who will give in to temptation and wickedness. That is why we must always be ready to act in the name of righteousness, to see the threat and stop it before it grows too powerful. I think that is what the Solar Exalted of old failed to do — they became complacent and did not recognize the corruption growing in their midst. They thought their battles won and put aside the duties the Unconquered Sun placed upon them. The world has paid a terrible price for their pride. It will not happen again.

Getting Righteous

It's the duty of the Zenith Caste to inspire and lead the people of the world to righteousness. But what is "righteousness" exactly? **Exalted** isn't intended to be an extended debate on morals or ethics, but it is a good idea to understand the cause that the Zeniths (and, to a degree, all of the Solar Exalted) fight for.

First, it's easy to say what righteousness is *not*. Righteousness isn't indulging in personal gratification at the expense of others. Things such as greed, theft, murder, rape and so forth are unrighteous, even wicked, acts. Many of the Dragon-Blooded can be seen as unrighteous for their indulgent and decadent ways. Righteousness is also not pale asceticism and self-denial, especially not turning your back on the world. The righteous aren't pacifists who hope and pray for deliverance, they're people who know what's right and act to uphold it, even at great cost.

Righteousness is acting with honor and justice and generally upholding the Virtues of **Exalted**: Compassion, Conviction, Temperance and Valor. For the Zenith Caste, it's more than just striving to live an upright life (which is important, too). The Resplendent Suns also try to guide other people to live righteously, by serving as examples, teaching where they can and punishing the wicked to show that they will not be tolerated in a righteous society. As Panther points out, it's not enough to *say* that you're righteous, you have to be willing to act according to your beliefs, and possibly even die for them, to be one of the Pillars of the Sun.

Ocean Pearl on Rebellion

When I overcame Blackheart in single combat, most of the crew of the *Scarlet Saber* came quickly over to my side, either because I'd liberated them from the rule of a heartless tyrant or because they feared me since I'd slain the man they thought was invincible. Those loyal to Blackheart either died in the fighting or were set adrift in a small launch, to fend for themselves and perhaps find their way to a port. I know that some of them did and that they began to spread tales of the woman who'd slain the Man With No Shadow. I'm sure some paint me as a demon temptress who worked her wiles over Blackheart before slaying him, but I don't much care, so long as they make it clear that I'm not an enemy to be taken lightly.

I suppose that I could have easily left the *Saber* once Blackheart was overcome. I'd only stayed as his captive, after all. But I found that once I held freedom in my hands, I was not so quick to leave behind the ship that had once been my prison and was now my home, nor the crew that was now mine to command. I love the freedom of the open seas, and I always have. So, should I have taken Blackheart's treasure, bought myself a stout cargo ship and begun ferrying goods among the islands and along the Great Inland Sea? Or should I have taken the booty, bought a fine house and some land and retired to a life of leisure, perhaps even found myself a husband or two like my parents would have wanted? That's what many sensible folk might have done, I suppose.

But I saw in the *Scarlet Saber* and my Exaltation a chance to do something more important. I was not chosen by the Unconquered Sun merely to liberate the crew and slaves of one ship, nor was I chosen so I could settle down and forget the glory of the Unconquered Sun's light and his words to me. The mutiny on board the *Saber* was only the beginning for me, and I knew it, although I doubt I could have put it into words then.

So, I gathered the crew on deck the next day, with the sun shining brightly overhead. All of them knew by then what I had become, so I let my anima shine around me as I spoke. I told them that any who wanted to were welcome to take a share of the booty and go ashore at the next port. But those who were willing to take on a challenge could stay with me. We would remain pirates,

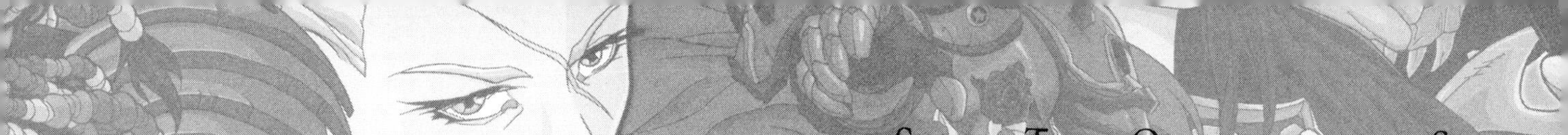

yes, but our prey would be the ships of the Realm, the Guild and the merchant houses that stripped the world of its wealth and dignity to fatten their own purses. Our booty would not be just jade and gold, but also the slaves we would free and the glory we would gain. People would tell tales of our exploits, and we would give back to them what they'd lost. Not just wealth, but honor, dignity and hope. I'm pleased to say that not one of my crew chose to leave at our next port, and I found others there willing to serve on board my ship.

My rules have always been simple ones. We raid the ships of the wealthy and the powerful, not honest folk, fishermen or travelers. We take prisoners only to ransom them, not to sell as slaves to the Guild or the Fair Folk. Part of the booty we take goes to the common people, the ones who need it most, while the rest is divided among the crew that won it. Those who surrender receive our mercy, while those who don't receive only the point of our blades. Our enemies are treated with respect, even if they do not always do us the same honor in return.

Some say that it is madness to attack the most powerful and wealthy ships, to show any mercy to their crews and, most of all, to give away anything that we take in our raids. I've heard these sentiments many times. After all, the smart pirate attacks smaller, less well-defended vessels, takes when he can, leaves no one alive to tell tales and holds on to what he has taken, yes? But I am not just any pirate, and my duty is not just to my crew and my own greed, it is to the Unconquered Sun that chose me and to the people.

We raid the ships of those who profit from the suffering and hard work of others, to show them that their gains will slip through their fingers. We make it difficult and expensive for the Realm's ships to bring tribute back to the Blessed Isle. We make it harder still for the Guild to profit in human misery and shipments of slaves and goods bought with blood. We strike them where it hurts the most, in their purses and their treasuries. The wealth we give back to the people of the islands helps to improve their lives far more than it would sitting in the counting-house of a Guild merchant or a Dragon-Blooded noble.

Oh, yes, the Realm and the Guild and the others we raid are powerful enemies, and any one of them would be happy to see my head mounted on a spike outside their palaces. I've heard that there are some substantial rewards out for the *Saber* and for me. This is proof that my existence is becoming quite expensive for my enemies, and it will become more expensive still. But I'm not just stealing from the wealthy because I can. I want to build something better than what is, and you can be sure that the Realm and the other powers in the world will fight to hold on to what they have. To make something new, we first have to tear down the old. We have to clear it away so there's a chance for the rest of us.

I'm not just a pirate. I'm a rebel against the Realm and all of its allies. Today, I sail my ship against merchant traders and tax collectors. Today, I give wealth back to the people. Tomorrow, I will have two ships, then five, then a dozen or more. I will strike raids against the powers of the world that will drawn their attention and their wrath, but I will weaken them in time. Then, the time will come when I will lead a fleet of ships against the Blessed Isle, when the people will rise up against the Realm and put an end to the rule of the Dragon-Blooded. That day is some time off, but I know that it will come eventually. For now, I work against the rulers of the world and inspire the people for the future.

Armattan on Justice

I tracked the raiders through the shifting dunes of the desert with Sirah at my side. Their trail led east, and I soon caught sight of a thin rivulet of smoke rising from a fire. As the sun sank into the distant sea at my back, painting the desert in shadows of red and orange, I climbed a low dune on my belly to look over it and down into the bandits' camp.

There were about a dozen of them, gathered around a small fire as the heat of the sun faded away. I could see a collection of goods taken from the caravan, and I sought out and spied the man who'd struck me down. I began to slide back from the crest of the dune when the cool metal of a blade touched my neck.

"What have we here?" said a voice from behind me. "A spy?" I turned over slowly to face the man who stood above me. I hadn't heard him approach. I glanced to the side and saw Sirah was missing before my eyes returned to the bandit looking down at me.

"You're just in time, desert rat," he said with a sneer twisting his mouth. "We could use a little entertainment tonight."

"I'll try to prove amusing," I said flatly, not moving as his sword pressed close against my exposed neck. "In fact, let me show you a trick."

"No tricks," the bandit said. "Stand up, slowly."

"Oh, you'll find this one interesting, I promise." Then there was a roar, and Sirah leapt from concealment and onto the bandit's back. He let out a scream and stumbled to the side as I flipped over the top of the dune and onto my feet. The men below us looked up at the sound of the cry as I drew my khatar from its sheath.

"Retribution is at hand!" I shouted, and Sirah bounded to my side, mouth wet with blood. I called on the Unconquered Sun for the strength I needed and felt my skin harden like iron as the fires burned within me. Then, I fell among the bandits like a blazing star. They drew blades and attacked, but their weapons were like pinpricks to me, while mine carried the force of my wrath with it. As we fought, I could feel light radiating from my forehead like a brand. Gradually, it grew to encompass my body in heatless

The Rule of Law

The Zenith Caste believes in the rule of law, after all, its members were the rulers and lawmakers of the Old Realm, and they know that a lawful society is the safest, most productive and most prosperous. But laws must be made to uphold righteousness and virtue, not the other way around. Unjust laws are made to be broken and overturned, just as unjust rulers must be defied and overthrown eventually. So, the members of the Zenith Caste see no conflict between righteousness and defying the laws of the Realm and its Dragon-Blooded rulers. Indeed, as they see it, the righteous *must* oppose them.

Resplendent Suns may foment rebellion against unrighteous rulers, incite mobs to riot against unfair laws, free slaves and raid ships and caravans belonging to the Realm, the Guild, the Deathlords or other enemies of righteousness. The wealth and goods the Zeniths seize help support their cause, while many of those they save from slavery or incite to rebel become their followers and supporters. The Realm and its allies brand these Exalted bandits, pirates and traitors and offer rewards for their capture or their heads.

The Zeniths aren't anarchists. They don't believe in rebellion for rebellion's sake. Most are fighting against injustice and tyranny in the world in hopes of building something better once the old structures have been torn down. Players and Storytellers should consider the long-term goals of the Zenith Caste (and the other Solar Exalted). What will they do when their current struggle for survival is over? If a character's goal is to overthrow the Realm, what comes next after that is achieved?

The Zeniths also know that their fight isn't going to be a quick or an easy one. The Dynasty has ruled the Realm for centuries, while other enemies, such as the Deathlords and their Malfean masters, are even older. Most also realize that the infrastructure of the Realm is all that holds Creation together. Outside in the Wyld lurk the forces of the Fair Folk and chaos, awaiting the opportunity to strike again. Sweeping away the old order en masse may give the Fair Folk just the opportunity they are looking for, so the Zenith must measure their actions carefully or else they may save the world from tyranny, only to see it drown in a tide of never-ending chaos and madness.

fire until the surviving bandits fell back from me and began to flee. Sirah pounced on one, pinning him to the ground, fulfilling my unspoken wish. The bandit's surviving companions fled into the desert, and I let them, knowing I could track them as I had before.

The bandit pinned by my feline friend was the one who had struck me down the day before, which seemed like a lifetime ago in my memory. The wound I'd given him along his arm was bandaged, half-concealed under his robe. I seized him and pressed my khatar against his throat.

"Now, my friend," I said, "I will have some answers from you." His eyes widened in terror, and he tried to choke out a reply, but all that came was a strangled gurgle. Finally, he managed to stammer.

"I... I cannot."

"You will," I said gravely, "or...."

"No," he shook his head feebly. "I *cannot*, I cannot betray the oath!" The fingers of his right hand uncurled, and I saw the sign branded there, an open eye in lines of red, faintly glowing in the shadows thrown by the fire. I recalled seeing it for a moment the previous day, before the darkness claimed me.

"The oath," he said. It was the oath sworn to the Perfect, the ruler of Paragon. I'd heard tales about Paragon, to the north, near the shore of the Great Inland Sea. Its ruler, known as the Perfect, wielded powerful magic, including the ability to exact an oath of allegiance from his people, an oath that resulted in a slow, painful death for whoever betrayed it. But we were far from Paragon, and these desert raiders looked like no citizens of any city.

In the end, the bandit did betray his oath, although I spared him the agony of his betrayal and granted him a quick and merciful death. It is likely more than he deserved. He told me how his people and other desert-folk became vassals of the Perfect, swearing the oath like the citizens of Paragon and serving its rulers wishes. Now, apparently, the Perfect wanted them to raid caravans traveling to Gem, to steal their cargoes of stones and firedust. It was clear to me that the Perfect had plans for the mines of the South and that he also had much to answer for.

Who appointed me arbiter of justice? The Unconquered Sun, in all of his wisdom. It is my experience that there may be law and order, but there is little justice in the world now. Not when rulers like the Perfect bind their people in the chains of a magical oath or when bandits rule in place of kings. "I offer you succor and place the power to seek justice in your hands," the Unconquered Sun said to me, and it is true. Our duty is to make the world a more righteous place, and one of the first steps toward that goal is to bring the wicked to justice, cutting the rot from the body of the world.

Over the days that followed my Exaltation, I tracked the remainder of the bandits through the desert and visited justice upon each of them but not before they told me all that they knew about the Perfect's plans, which, unfortunately, was very little. I knew that one day I would have to deal with the Perfect and his goals for the South, but before that day came, I still had much to learn about my gifts and my duty. So, after my work in the desert was done, I made my way north and west, with the gems I recovered lining my pockets and Sirah at my heels. I knew I could not return to Gem yet, since no one would believe my tale and would likely think that I had betrayed and killed my fellow travelers to steal the stones for myself.

Instead, I made my way to the Lap first, to lose myself among the people there. I provided aid where I could, studied and learned more and watched carefully for signs of trouble. I met another like me there. He was a tired-looking man, worn and rugged from the road, but one of the greatest fighters I had ever seen. I helped him escape when he drew the attention of the Dragon-Blooded and learned from him there were others like us — not many, but enough that we found each other from time to time. That was when I decided to leave the Lap and return to Gem. I offered for him to travel with me, but my Dawn brother had other plans and bid me farewell.

I decided I would seek out others like myself, the Chosen of the Unconquered Sun, and help them understand their purpose. Together, we could accomplish far more than any of us could alone. Accomplish what? Why, the salvation of the world, of course. I know that sounds like a lot, but it's a matter of taking things one step at a time, as I have. Sometimes, individuals do get the chance to save the whole of Creation, like the Scarlet Empress did when she threw back the Fair Folk, but most of the time, it's a matter of helping one person or one village at a time. Those deeds add up, and when you look back on them, it's amazing what you can accomplish, what we can accomplish, together.

Fire Orchid on Leadership

The thing I have learned about heroism is that dealing with the immediate threat is often the easiest part of the job. When the Fair Folk threatened Masi and my home, I didn't give much thought to what I was doing in challenging them. When I leapt from my burning house, all I was concerned with was driving them off and reaching safety. It's after you've won the victory or driven off the enemy that things start to get complicated.

So there I was, my home in flames, an awed and stunned boy at my side, with the village suffering some damage from the arrival of Hayashi and his troupe. I'd heard the voice of the Unconquered Sun speaking to me, could feel the power still seething inside me, the power that had allowed me to survive and drive off the raiders — for the time being at least. I knew better than most what it meant, for me and for those around me. I could not

Administering Justice

In the First Age, the members of the Zenith Caste were the judges and the arbiters of justice. They saw to it that the guilty were punished and the innocent protected and ensured that the punishment for wrongdoing fit the crime. In the Second Age, the Pillars of the Sun are forced to carry out their duties without the support of the Realm or its laws, which have declared them outlaws and Anathema. Still, that does not change the fact that justice is one of the duties of the Zenith Caste, and there is certainly a great need for justice in the world.

Some Zeniths answer the cry for justice by finding and punishing wrongdoers, particularly those the law cannot (or will not) touch. The bandits who rob a village, only to be found slain the next day, the stolen goods returned. The killer who stalks from the shadows, only to vanish and menace others no more. The cruel despot overthrown by a stranger. These things and many others are the work of the Zenith Caste pursuing justice.

But justice is not just a matter of punishing crimes. It is also about seeing that the right thing is done; that each person receives what is his or her due. In the eyes of the Zenith Caste, the natural order of the world has been upset, with bandits and despots ruling over nations and the Celestial Exalted exiled from their rightful place. The Pillars of Heaven seek justice for themselves as well as for the rest of the world, especially for the terrible wrong done to them at the end of the First Age.

remain in Rana. I would have to move before word of what happened reached the Immaculate Order and the officials of the Realm, before the Wyld Hunt came looking for me. But I knew that with the disappearance of the Scarlet Empress it might be some time before the Hunt was gathered. Even isolated as I was, I had some inkling of the goings-on in the Realm. The Scarlet Houses were in disarray, circling each other warily like jackals over a kill.

More important was the future of the village of Rana. Yes, I had driven off the Fair Folk, and Masi had already begun talking, babbling on about my heroism and the amazing deeds I'd performed. But what about when Hayashi returned, as I knew that he would? I could remain and face him again, but Hayashi was no fool. He would come with a greater force than before. Perhaps I could stand against it, but could Rana? I needed to lead danger away from the village, not directly to it, but I couldn't leave the villagers helpless, either.

There was nothing to salvage from my villa. It was a part of my old life, a life of quiet and contentment that I thought was mine, but it wasn't and probably never will be. Once a soldier, always a soldier, as they say. So, I let my villa burn (easy, given that there was nothing I could do about it), took Masi in tow and headed for the village proper to see what damage had been done.

It wasn't as bad as I'd expected; some homes burned and a few dead, one house transformed into a strange sort of tree, its timbers sinking roots into the ground, putting forth leaves and growing wicked spikes that had impaled an old man, Rising Star. The headman of the village, a florid, red-faced Easterner named Certan, rushed up to us as we approached the square.

"Madame General!" he said breathlessly. He always insisted on addressing me like some displaced nobility, although I didn't care for it. "Thank the Immaculate Dragons and all the gods you are safe!"

I smiled thinly. "Only one god had anything to do with my safety, Certan." At that, it was as if a dam burst and words came spilling from Masi in a flood. He proceeded to tell the entire tale of his rush to warn me of the Fair Folk's attack, how I fended off their leader with nothing more than a hoe and of our escape from my burning villa. He told in great detail how I magically donned my armor and drove off the Fair Folk with a fearsome display of sword fighting, acting out each thrust and parry as he told it (and I became certain that the tale would grow with each and every telling). Certan was quite impressed, to say the least, and looked at me like a gift descended from Heaven.

"Oh, wondrous lady," he said, "we are in your debt! Surely with you here, the Fair Folk will not be so quick to attack again. You will drive them off and—"

"No," I said, and the headman's speech skidded to a halt like a dog trying to stop on a polished marble floor.

"Wha…?" he managed to stumble out. "N… no?"

"No," I repeated. "I won't always be here to drive off the Fair Folk, Certan. My home is burning and will soon be nothing but ash. All that I have is what you see with me. I have a purpose in this world, a duty I must fulfill, and I cannot do so by remaining here."

"But… but we will build you a new home!" Certan said, looking like he was near tears. "A palace! We will gift you with livestock and the finest of the harvest, with whatever we have, but please, I beg you, do not abandon us in our time of need!"

"Certan, be still. Who said anything about abandoning you? I said only that I won't always be here to fight your battles for you. You must learn to do that for yourselves, but I am willing to teach you that much, at least." And so began my work in teaching the folk of Rana the arts of war.

It was no simple task. They were citizens of a petty kingdom that, like so many others, forbade its citizens from bearing arms, for an armed and trained populace does not need to fear outside threats so much, nor is it so easily inclined to bow head to oppressive taxes. So, I helped give Rana a measure of independence.

The Unconquered Sun gave me two tasks in my Exaltation: "strike down the unrighteous with your fury, and guide others with your wisdom." I see the second as more important than the first. It's one thing to travel about smiting monsters and fending off those who prey on the helpless and the innocent and quite another to guide the people of the world, to create a real change in their lives. I think the conceit of the Realm and the Dragon-Blooded was to make the people of the Threshold dependent on them. It served their purpose well, since it kept power in the hands of the Dynasty and their legions. But I have no desire to rule like the Dragon-Blooded have done. If I am to guide others with my insight, then let it be toward a goal that makes them more able to care for themselves. There will always be tasks too great for any single person, but I believe there is nothing beyond the reach of a people who act together for a common cause.

So I taught the people of Rana, formed a militia and showed them how to fight against enemies great and small. I also planted the seeds of how to teach others, so they could maintain what I began. I understand that young Masi wants nothing more than to be a militiaman one day, and I suspect that he'll be a good one. When Hayashi and his band returned, as I knew they would, I stood with allies at my back as well. That day, the Fair Folk learned Rana would not be easy prey for them in the future, and I left them with one other gift. I marked Hayashi in battle with the wound that drove him from the field (thought I regret to say that I did not slay him). I am certain that he will not forget the injury but that he will give little mind to a small village in the Threshold, putting his attention instead on obtaining his revenge against the "old woman" who defeated him twice. I suppose, one day, Rana will send the tax collector packing as well, and a well-deserved banishment it will be given that the town's rulers had never given it anything but tax assessments and conscription notices.

So, we Zeniths teach and guide others to deal with those dangers in the world that they can and take the threats that are too great for them upon ourselves, which is just as it should be. As I try to tell the youngsters who make up the rest of my Circle, it is not enough for us to battle and overcome if we do not also build and leave things better than when we found them.

Wind on Truth

Raiton flew through the twisting streets of Gethamane like his namesake, and I followed, the buildings and the turnings blurring past as I ran and leapt like never before. The white and golden glow around me lit my way through the darkness, brighter than a torch or lantern. It showed the startled faces of the few people who poked their heads out of doors and windows to see what was going on and, just as quickly, ducked back in, to close and lock the portals behind them.

I don't know for certain how long we ran, my thoughts were focused only on keeping Raiton in sight, since I had many questions for the mysterious visitor. My mind was in

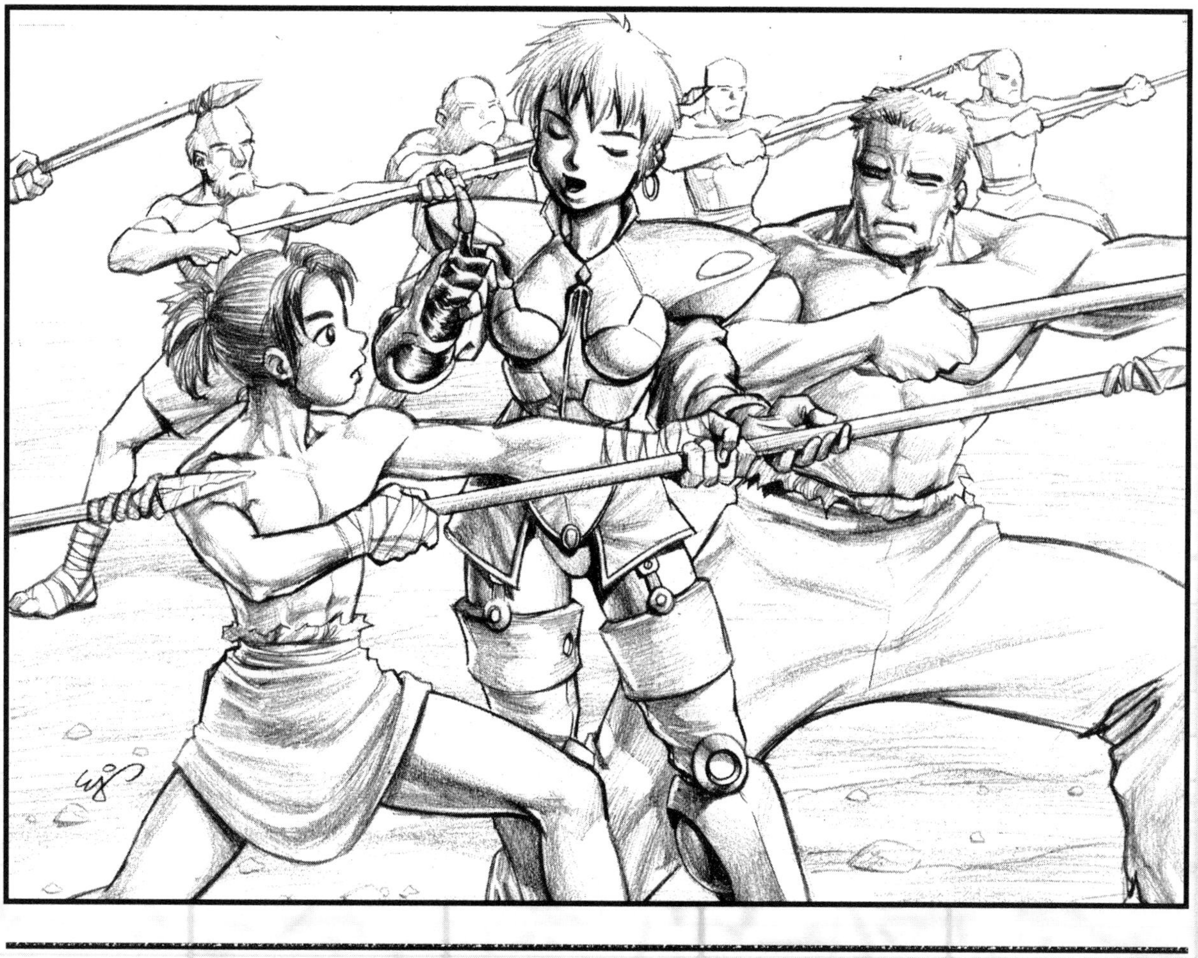

Leaders and Followers

The Zenith Exalted are born leaders, and part of their purpose is to guide others, both their fellow Exalted and mortals, toward a better life. They can encourage others toward virtuous and righteous behavior and also inspire confidence and self-reliance.

Zeniths tend to have followers (and the Followers Background) more than any other Solar Caste. It's part of their nature to gain the attention and the loyalty of others. Some Resplendent Suns accept this responsibility easily and choose to gather their followers around them. These Exalts create cults and mercenary companies, found villages and towns or else are chosen to lead or even rule places far enough from the Realm that the Wyld Hunt doesn't threaten them. The Zeniths attempt to be fair and just leaders, guiding their people toward righteousness and directing them against their enemies.

Other Zeniths prefer to lead by example and rhetoric but do not take on followers. These Golden Bulls prefer not to be tied down to a particular place or to deal with the difficulties of leading and providing for a large following. Instead, they travel far and wide (often in the company of a Circle), carrying the message of the Unconquered Sun and providing guidance to others in times of need. When the crisis is passed and they have done what they can to ensure the people can fend for themselves, these Zeniths move on, always just ahead of the Wyld Hunt and their other enemies, leaving behind them stories of their legendary deeds.

Storytellers may want to consider the size of followings allowed for Exalted characters in the series (both for Zeniths and other castes). Some series are better suited to large groups of followers than others, and players should adjust their character concepts accordingly.

turmoil over what had passed between us, over the terrible creature that had attacked Gentle Song and over the way that I had helped to slay it. When Raiton finally came to rest, I saw that we were in a ruined and abandoned part of the city. The light around me cast dark shadows amidst crumbling walls of stone overgrown with mountain lichen and mosses.

Raiton cocked his head, as if listening to some sound I couldn't hear. Then, he turned toward me, his expression unreadable, his eyes mysterious.

"They will come for you soon enough," he said, "the Wyld Hunt." I felt a chill shudder through my limbs, and the fullness of my fate began to weigh upon me.

"What have you done to me?" I said, my quavering voice barely above a whisper, although I wanted to shout, to grab the dark stranger by his shoulders and shake him.

"I have saved your life," Raiton said quietly, "as I failed to do so long ago. It is a debt I have carried since then."

"What do you mean?" I asked. "We only met a few nights ago."

Raiton looked at me for a moment, and I could feel a sense of… longing, as his eyes lingered on mine. Then, he looked away. "My debt is paid. You must leave Gethamane before the Realm's hounds come for you, oh, Resplendent Sun. It will be dawn soon enough."

"What did you call me?"

"One of your many titles. You are among the Chosen of the Unconquered Sun, and I suspect that you have much work ahead of you, if you escape from the children of our betrayers. Farewell." A single, graceful leap took him up to the top of the wall four yards above our heads, his cloak spreading around him like wings.

"Wait!" I said. "You can't just leave me here! I need your help!"

Raiton looked down at me and something unreadable flashed across his face. "And you received it," he said. "My debt is paid, and we are even. Perhaps we will meet again."

He spread his cloak, and the shadows flowed around him. The cloak became wings as Raiton shrank into the form of his namesake. His shadow passed across the bright face of the Moon, his caw echoed against the cold stones, and he was gone. I stood among the ruins alone, surrounded by a fire that gave me no warmth.

"Don't look to *him* for any more help," said a voice from behind me.

I spun to face the stranger, my sword raised to fend off an attack. The golden light revealed a woman standing close behind me. She was smaller than me, smaller even than Gentle Song, with a round face and a wide, flat nose. Her dark hair was braided at the nape of her neck, and her wide eyes were the rich color of the fine amber that gleamed from her ears, as was the tunic she wore over a loose-fitting pair of dull-orange pants. A wooden walking staff rested lightly in her hands.

"Be at ease," she said to me, holding out an open hand. "I am no threat to you. I am here to help you. My name is Sula."

"Help me?" I said somewhat dumbly, the sudden burst of energy draining from my limbs. "No one can help me," I said, shaking my head, feeling the tears begin to well up in my eyes as the enormity of my fate fell upon me. "I must meditate and pray to the Immaculate Dragons for their guidance, hope for forgiveness…" I began to drop into the First Lotus Position, but Sula's hand shot out and roughly grabbed my shoulder.

"Sitting and praying isn't going to help you!" she said. "You need to move! You glow brighter than a torch, boy! It won't take long for them to find you, even out here. You need to get out of sight and give your anima time to dim. I know a safe place, if you're willing to trust me."

"Why should I?" I said, pulling away from her grasp. "How do I know that you're not a spirit come to lure me into some dark tunnel and devour me?"

"Listen to your heart," she said, "but if it helps, I swear upon the names of Gaia and Luna, the Five Maidens and the Unconquered Sun. If my words are not the truth, may I suffer their anger for my lies." Although she swore in the names of gods that the Immaculates had forbidden to the lips of the unExalted, it was as though I could feel the weight of her words, and I knew it was not an oath taken lightly.

"Alright," I said, "show me the way."

Sula helped me to hide and, eventually, to leave Gethamane behind. She also taught me who and what I was. She told me she belonged to the Cult of the Illuminated. I had heard of them but had always dismissed them as a minor heresy found in the Threshold. But the cult held to the belief that the Exalted, those who the Immaculate Order labels Anathema, are, in truth, the foreordained saviors of all Creation. The sutras of the Illuminated Ones tell us "In the time of greatest despair for the Realm, there will come those who wear the light of the sun as if it were a mantle. They will bring light into the darkness and show the way to righteousness and eternal bliss."

They also say, "The Illuminated Ones carry the legacy of the First Age, made pure and whole once again, so that they may restore all of Creation." Sula says that I and others like me partake of the Essence of the Solar Exalted, who became corrupt in the First Age and were slain by the Dragon-Blooded for their hubris. The Unconquered Sun has granted us the blessing of their power so that we can undo the harm that has been done to the world. Now, it is the Dragon-Blooded whose false and overweening pride draws the anger of the Incarna.

Sula herself is one of the Sidereal Exalted, the Chosen of the Five Maidens, who stand behind the Cult of the Illuminated and guide its hands. She is a Chosen of the Maiden of Journeys, and she explained to me how her horoscopes and divinations guided her to me. As the Sidereals advised the Solar Exalted in the Old Realm, so Sula advised and taught me. As I learned, my fear of what I had become changed. I no longer fear the gifts I was given. Instead, I fear for the Realm and all Creation, if we do not unite to stand against the forces that threaten us.

To do that, we must bring the truth to the people and the world. The Dragon-Blooded have concealed the truth through their rule and through the Immaculate Philosophy, which teaches that they are the closest to spiritual perfection. They forbid the worship of the Incarna, and they hunt down the reborn Celestial Exalted to eliminate any threat to their reign. We must show the world that we are not the demons we are made out to be, but the Chosen of the gods, here to lead the way to a new golden age.

It will not be easy to convince people of the truth. I had a difficult time accepting it myself, and I heard the Unconquered Sun's voice, felt the power within me. I know that the Immaculate Order and the Dragon-Blooded will call us monsters, Anathema, and say that we are only trying to deceive, but we will demonstrate the truth to the world through our words and our deeds.

The Whole Truth

Of course, Wind doesn't know the *whole* truth about things. In fact, few of the Solar Exalted do. Although they are gifted with power and insight by the Unconquered Sun, the Solar Exalted (and the Zeniths in particular) aren't necessarily privy to all the secrets of Creation. In fact, most Solars are still very much in the process of learning who and what they are, piecing together fragmentary memories and dreams of the First Age, discovering their own abilities and exploring the past.

Wind is better informed than many Solars, but even he doesn't know that the Sidereal Exalted are actually behind the Immaculate Order as well as the Cult of the Illuminated or that the Sidereals were the ultimate authors of the overthrow of the Solar Exalted in the First Age. Part of the work of the Zenith Caste is discovering the truth about the world. But Exalted are still fallible, and they may come to believe things that aren't true, like the doctrines of the Cult of the Illuminated or those of the Immaculate Order. They also sometimes act on these mistaken beliefs.

Storytellers should remind players to separate what they know (from reading the **Exalted** book and other sourcebooks, such as this one) from what their characters know. Storytellers should also feel free change the truth to suit their own series and to provide players with a few surprises from time to time. For example, imagine discovering that the Sidereal Exalted had nothing to do with the downfall of the Solars, it being instead a secret alliance between the Dragon-Blooded and the Deathlords!

There are many layers of truth in **Exalted**. For example, although Wind knows that the Terrestrial Exalted rebelled against the Solars, he doesn't know about the role the Sidereals played or their reasons. He also doesn't know about the role of the Lunar Exalted in the downfall of the Solars or other facts the Gold faction of the Sidereal Exalted finds inconvenient. Let the discovery of one truth reveal even more mysteries for the characters to uncover, and never let them forget that information is only as reliable as the source it comes from.

Chapter Three
The World Awaiting Us

The Zenith Caste is by no means united in its views or opinions. Although the Zeniths carry the message of the Unconquered Sun and believe in upholding righteousness, they don't always agree on the best means of doing so or on how to deal with the forces arrayed against them in the world.

Like all Solars, the Zeniths quickly learn to respect the power of the Dragon-Blooded and the Realm. The Scarlet Houses and the Wyld Hunt still try to murder any Solar Exalted they discover, so the Zeniths must tread carefully where the Dragon-Blooded are concerned. Although many of the Hammers of Heaven would like nothing better than to bring down the Manses of the Dragon-Blooded, raze the Palace Sublime and rebuild the Imperial City from the ruins, they know that the Realm is powerful and they are few. For now the Blessed Isle is far too dangerous a place for any of the Solar Exalted to walk openly.

Many Zeniths hold out hope for even the Dragon-Blooded, recalling the days when they faithfully served the Celestial Exalted and helped keep the Old Realm safe from harm. Some believe that once the corruption is rooted out of the Realm and its houses that the remaining Dragon-Blooded can be restored to their proper place in the world. Of course, some point out that, having tasted power for so long, the Terrestrial Exalted may not easily return to their role as servants.

Although their views of the world are shaped by their Exaltation and the wisdom imparted to them by the Unconquered Sun, the Resplendent Suns all begin their existences as ordinary humans and are shaped by their experiences prior to the Second Breath. Those from the Threshold have usually seen hardship, either in the form of Fair Folk and barbarian raids or from oppressive rulers who keep their domains safe at the cost of liberty and human suffering. This often makes the Zeniths ill-disposed to both the rulers of the Threshold and the forces that lie beyond the edges of Creation. Those Pillars of the Sun who hail from the Realm itself must often struggle with self-doubt and exile from their home, since they are labeled Anathema and stalked by the Wyld Hunt.

When you first create your Zenith character, take time to consider how the character's background and life before taking the Second Breath influence relations with the other factions and people of the world. The tales of the Exalted in the earlier chapters of this book affect the views they offer here, an example of the range of opinions found among the Pillars of the Sun.

Panther

The Scavenger Lands

If you would see the future of the world, I'd say look no further than the Scavenger Lands. Not that I think the Lands represent our future fate as they are now, but they hold the seeds of a greater future, if we cultivate them properly. My Circle is united in its desire to free the Threshold from the rule of the Realm, and the Scavenger Lands are the ideal place for us to start.

First, these lands never swore allegiance to the Realm or the Dragon-Blooded. A glimmer of the pride of the Old Realm remains here, in the place that was once its heartland. Although the Blessed Isle may have been the head of the Old Realm, the East was its heart, and the heart is stronger at bearing hardship than the head. The Scavenger Lands are still fertile and rich, although ravaged by the Great Contagion like everywhere else. Many people have moved here to farm the land and build new towns and villages.

The Scavenger Lands have two great challenges that we Exalted can face, one from without and the other from within. The region faces threats from outside, particularly from the Fair Folk and the Deathlords. The Deathlord Mask of Winters has already taken Thorns, his forces poised to enter the Scavenger Lands from the south. To the east, near the Elemental Pole of Wood, lie Wyld places. Fair Folk and barbarians raid and plunder almost at will, with none to challenge them but ill-prepared local militias and us. If the Scavenger Lands are to prosper, they must be protected from the forces that would invade and conquer them or those that would simply strip them clean and leave nothing but bones and living husks with the dreams torn from their souls. Already, my Circle has confronted raiders and negotiated with the Mask of Winters, and I have heard of other Exalted doing much the same.

The Scavenger Lands also face danger from within, and this is the greater of the two challenges. Although they have potential, the Lands are not united, and they must unite if they are to become a power to challenge the Realm and the rule of the Dragon-Blooded. In Nexus, in the arena, I thought only about myself — how I would survive to see my next sunrise. Many people in the Scavenger Lands and the Threshold think this way. Nexus is a prime example. The city is like a beast: thinking only of feeding its hunger, finding a mate to rut with and fighting off any that invade its territory. It is blind to ideals of justice, honor and righteousness, and it is our duty to open its eyes, and the eyes of all people, to guide them back onto the right path. Much the same is true of the other cities and towns of the River Province.

In my experience, people react to hardship in one of two ways. The first is to turn inward and protect themselves, hardening against the suffering of others so they can survive. That is what happened to most of the folk of the Scavenger Lands — and the world. People in Nexus mind their own business and step over strangers bleeding in the streets rather than risking their own necks. But the other way people react to hardship is to come together, to unite and become greater than they were before. They care for each other, and their suffering is like a crucible, burning away the impure and creating something fine and precious. The Scavenger Lands are a crucible, and we, the Chosen of the Unconquered Sun, are the flames that purify.

The Realm

The Realm is only a shadow of its former glory, but it is still worthy of our respect, if not our allegiance. The Dragon-Blooded have held the Blessed Isle for centuries and ruled the Realm with a strong hand, at least until the Scarlet Empress disappeared, breaking the unity of the houses and setting them at each others throats. The Dragon-Bloods have also maintained the Wyld Hunt, which, for centuries, has slain any of our kind returning to the world. All it will take is for the Scarlet Houses to unite behind a new ruler for the Wyld Hunt to regain its full strength and for the Dragon-Blooded to turn their attention toward us again. However, this time, they will not find us frightened and confused, newly reborn into the world.

Although the rulers of the Realm have declared themselves our enemies, not all of the Dragon-Blooded need to be. I have fought with as well as against the Terrestrial Exalted, and they are worthy allies when they choose to uphold what is righteous. Some of the outcastes in the East and elsewhere in the Threshold care little for the politics of the Realm, and they may come to support us. Even the great houses may do so, once the corruption within them have been cut out and we have shown them the error of their ways.

The most corrupt of the Dragon-Blooded are the ones who have set aside their traditional role and try to be something they are not. The Terrestrial Exalted were made by the Elemental Dragons to be soldiers, not rulers. They are excellent warriors, but their rule is based on a soldier's understanding of rulership. They rule by strength alone, unguided by wisdom or understanding of higher principles. Even the rule of the Scarlet Empress was based on her power to enter the Imperial Manse and repel the invasion of the Fair Folk and on the power she gathered in the years that followed. Power without guidance, without higher purpose, turns to tyranny, and it will not be easy to convince the Dragon-Blooded to give up the power they have taken.

The Wyld

Our misguided brothers who rule the Blessed Isle are a challenge to overcome, but even they are nothing compared to the power of the Wyld and that which lies beyond the gates of Creation. The Wyld is chaos and madness, and all that dwell there are infected with it. It stands like a roaring river, only barely held back from the fields of Creation by a weakening dam. For now, we can only rush from place to place, shoring up the dam when it leaks and madness pours into the world. In time, we will have to strengthen the dam and build its walls higher, or the Wyld will drown us all.

The creatures of the Wyld are dangerous because their only purpose is to tear down and destroy what we build. The Dragon-Blooded and the Realm are foes we can understand; they seek to conquer and rule. The Wyld barbarians seek only to destroy. The Fair Folk feed on our dreams and our souls. There can be no real parlay with them, any more than one can forge a lasting peace with storm or plague. We can only fight them when they appear and force them back where they came from. If we do not, then civilization — and, perhaps, all Creation — is doomed.

Of greatest concern in the Wyld are the Lunar Exalted. They were once our partners and allies, helping guide Creation and the Old Realm. They suffered much at the end of the First Age, and those that dwell now in the Wyld seek vengeance for the wrongs done them. But allowing the Lunars to raze cities and nations and sew chaos is not justice, and their misguided attacks must be stopped. Dace believes there is some hope for the Lunars, that we can reason with them and perhaps even reclaim them from the Wyld. I hope that he is right, but we cannot allow our hopes to prevent us from doing what we must to defend the Threshold and its people. Any Lunar who sends beastmen and barbarians to raid and pillage must answer to my Circle and to me.

The Shadowlands

When Swan and the others of my Circle proposed an alliance with the Deathlord Mask of Winters, I opposed it, and I oppose it still. No matter how well Swan handled negotiations with the new ruler of Thorns and no matter how useful the Deathlord's support may be to our work in the Scavenger Lands, I say that no good can come of alliances with the Deathlords and their kind.

As much as the Fair Folk and the things of the Wyld, the Deathlords represent a disruption of the natural order. The dead must move on from this world to what awaits them, or else, there will soon be no room in the world for the living. As a priest of the Unconquered Sun, it is my duty to bring light into the darkness and to lay hungry ghosts and walking dead to rest. Our "alliance" may buy us valuable time to deal with more pressing matters, but mark my words, sooner of later, the Mask of Winters will turn on his supposed "allies," and we will not be able to strike first without violating the agreement we have made. For now, we can only hope to be prepared when the Deathlord chooses to act.

For the Deathlord's minions, living and unliving, I feel only pity. The restless dead should be allowed some solace and the means to pass on, while the living should not be condemned to live like the dead before their time. The so-called Abyssal Exalted who serve the Deathlords are a mystery. They are like our dark reflections. Where did they come from, and what is their purpose? These are things we must know, if we are to deal with them some day.

Other Solar Exalted

It is important for us to have allies in our struggle for righteousness. Fortunately, the Unconquered Sun provides, and each of his Chosen has a special strength. Apart, we are powerful, but united, there is nothing we cannot accomplish. I'm lucky to be part of a Perfect Circle, with members of each caste complimenting each other and making the whole greater than the sum of its parts. There are times, of course, when I don't agree with my brothers and sisters, but we discuss all matters in the open and choose our actions as a group.

Within the Circle, it is my duty to always remind my brothers and sisters of the cause that we serve, to help inspire them. They, in turn, often remind me of the harsh realities we face and the ways we can deal with them. As my sister Harmonious Jade says, "When you turn your face to the sun, it's wise to have someone standing in your shadow, watching your back."

Ocean Pearl

Mortals

I don't much care for the term "mortal." It sounds like a term the Dragon-Blooded would use, or the Deathlords. After all, I may live for a very long time, but I may die tomorrow under a enemy's blade. I'm really just as mortal as anyone in the ways that really matter. I breathe, I fight, I love, I hate, and I prefer the company of "mortals" to most of the immortals and Exalted I've met.

I know that my crew and many people in the islands look up to me and respect me. I also know that more than a few of them fear me. Would that be any different if I was just an infamous pirate captain? Perhaps, but it's not so different. I do what I think is right for my crew and the people, and they understand that. After all, I chose to mutiny against Blackheart before the Unconquered Sun chose me, when I was just a "mortal." My power may have let me overcome him, but I would have made the effort anyway.

The way I see it, most people are decent enough. If you treat them well and give them a good example, they follow it. The crew that knows it's earning a share in the booty works that much harder for it. If you treat your shipmates like slaves, then, sooner or later, they will rebel. That's what I did, and I'll see to it that any slavers I encounter find the business of selling flesh *far* more expensive than they thought.

The Deathlords

The Deathlords are a force to reckon with, make no mistake. The Bodhisattva Anointed by Dark Water is a power in the West and among the islands and is none too pleased with me for killing Blackheart. Well, that and a few raids against ships entering and leaving the Skullstone Archipelago, which earned us a fair haul along with the Deathlord's anger.

The Bodhisattva has placed a bounty on the *Scarlet Saber* and me and also sent some of his minions to plague us. When the Knight of Ghosts and Shadows captured my first mate, Tanar, while we were in port, I followed them back to Onyx on Darkmist to rescue the man. There, I got a firsthand look at the rule of a Deathlord, and I didn't like what I saw.

The buildings were carved from black rock, the streets filled with people so somber it was difficult to tell the dead from the living. Not all of them were dead, though. Onyx puts its dead to work, so there were skeletal footmen and bearers, sometimes with their bones elaborately carved and gilded, and zombies swathed in heavy cloth, wearing masks to cover their faces. The people of Onyx live in luxury because the dead do most of the work, but I suppose they pay the piper when their time comes to die and they're put to work as well.

It was in Onyx that I first discovered a Solar Exalted working for the Deathlords. While I was there, I spotted Moray Darktide. I'd heard tales about him and wondered if he was one of us. I was disappointed to discover that he was, rather than one of the Deathlords' Abyssal Exalted, a member of the Dawn Caste. Fortunately, he didn't spot me when I made my way from the docks to the Bodhisattva's brooding palace.

Tanar would be the first to say that stealth isn't my greatest talent, but I still knew some ways to get into the palace. If you can't avoid drawing attention, sometimes, the best thing you can do is get as much attention as possible. So, I dressed provocatively, with my face veiled in shimmering silk, and approached the palace as a dancing girl looking to make a few coins. It wasn't hard to interest the Deathlord's living guards in some entertainment not composed of dry bones or rotting flesh, and I'd learned a thing or two working in seaside taverns. Plus, I can dance as no ordinary woman can — my Charms fired the hearts and loins of the soldiers until they were almost panting with lust, as I danced and swayed past them, trailing brightly colored scarves.

One of them quickly took me aside, and a blade pressed against his throat was enough to convince him to take me down to the dungeons. Then, I relieved the jailer of his keys and his life with a single stroke of my blade. Thank the Unconquered Sun for Tanar's strangled warning as I got him free or the sweep of a soulsteel blade would have taken my head off. I rolled to the side, my own sword in my hand, to face the Knight of Ghosts and Shadows. The man is beautiful, but it's a darkling beauty: flesh pale and cold as marble, hair black as night, brow marked with a midnight sun. He's the only Abyssal Exalted I've encountered, and I hope not to meet any more of them. He fought like a demon, but he made the mistake of underestimating Tanar, who distracted him long enough for me to stun him and for us to make good our escape.

We took skeletal horses from the Deathlord's own stables. They are utterly obedient to their riders but unsettling to ride, all clattering bones held together with spun wire. We rode like mad on our stolen mounts and reached the harbor well ahead of our pursuit, turning a corner to see a stocky man with blue-gray skin and pale blue hair, his silken shirt blowing in the wind. He wore a breastplate of gleaming orichalcum and was flanked by a pair of zombie sailors: Moray Darktide, captain of the *Mailed Fist*.

Solar Exalted

"Leaving our fair island so soon?" Darktide said in a mocking tone, a naked blade in his hands, gleaming in the fading sun. The zombies carried swords, held at the ready.

"I think I've enjoyed enough of its hospitality," I replied.

"Oh, but you haven't even begun to sample its many wonders," he said, taking a few steps closer, a smirk twisting his face. "Like me, for example."

"I'm not very impressed so far."

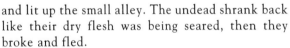

"Allow me the opportunity to change that," he said. Then, he sprang, like a saber-toothed hunting cat.

The leap threw me from my mount, but I rolled with it, planting a foot in Darktide's stomach and flipping him over my head to roll onto the cobblestones. We both rolled to our feet as my sword came clear of its sheath, just in time to block the pirate captain's attack, sparks of Essence leaping from our blades.

"Nicely done," he said. "You fight well."

"You haven't seen the half of it," I replied. But in truth, Darktide was more than a match for me. He struck, I parried, but he didn't allow me the opportunity to take the offensive, slowly forcing me back against the side of the alley. I saw his zombies closing on Tanar, their swords raised. I wanted to tell him to run, but he didn't know where our boat was concealed.

I blocked another of Darktide's strikes, but then, he slipped through my guard and his sword scraped against my skin. Were it not for my Charms, the blow might have been fatal. As it was, it hurt like pure fire, and Darktide laughed in triumph.

"First blood to me!" he crowed.

That was when my anima flared around me and I struck, not at Darktide, but at his zombies. The flames burning around me drove away the darkness and lit up the small alley. The undead shrank back like their dry flesh was being seared, then they broke and fled.

"What are you...?" Darktide began, glancing toward where his crewmen once stood. That distraction was enough of an opportunity, and I struck with all my strength, slamming him into the far wall. I would have preferred to finish him, but there was no time; the Deathlord's forces were not far behind us, and more of Darktide's zombies could have appeared at any moment, so we fled.

It should be no great wonder that I'm careful not to embrace all of my Solar brothers and sisters right away. I've learned the hard way that not all of the Chosen of the Unconquered Sun further the cause of righteousness in the world. I've since encountered Solars worthy of the name and of my respect, but my encounter with Moray Darktide showed me there are those of us who have lost their way. It is up to us Zeniths to show them the error of their ways or else send their Essence on to find a more suitable vessel. The loss of a Solar in battle is a tragedy, but the loss of one of us to corruption is far worse.

It's thanks to men such as Moray Darktide that the Deathlords have come to know the value of having the

Solar Exalted in their service, whatever their patron or caste. But I can tell you this, no Deathlord will ever have me, in life or in death, of that you can be certain.

The Dragon-Blooded

The rulers of their houses may laze about enjoying their pleasures, but the kin they send to sea are hardy enough. Most of the Dragon-Bloods I've encountered have been from House V'neef and House Peleps, and I can almost believe that, like the stories say, some of them truly have ice water in their veins instead of blood. The Peleps especially are fierce sailors — good fighters, too. Odds are the captain of an imperial ship is Dragon-Blooded and an Aspect of Water, though the merchant ships don't always have Terrestrial Exalted aboard, just enough of them do to keep things interesting.

I've heard tales and seen things that say the Dragon-Blooded usurped the Old Realm from us, the Celestial Exalted. That may well be, but whether they did or not, they're certainly making a mess of it now. They call for as much tribute as ever from the Threshold and the islands: jade, coral, silver and silk to fatten the coffers of the Scarlet Houses, and for what? So they can buy more legions and mercenaries to strengthen their own claim to the throne? So they can throw more lavish parties and poison a few more rivals? And when the people of the islands or the Threshold need the aid of their "divine protectors," you can be sure that the Realm will send the worst they've got in hopes of being rid of them.

That's one of the reasons I find it hard to hate the Dragon-Blooded who find their way out here. Odds are they're either not interested in the political struggles of the Blessed Isle or they were sent here as some sort of exile or punishment. They try to do their duty without much support, but all the same, I don't let any sympathy for their plight keep me from plundering their ships. I've faced my share of the scions of the Realm on the high seas and on dry land as well, and I can tell you that the Dragon-Blooded are no foes to laugh at — not unless you want to get them angry and careless, that is.

The West

Ah, the islands of the West. They have been my home for all of my life, and yet, I find that I am only beginning to understand them. They're a collection of the best and worst of humanity. They're home to pirates and raiders, some of them folk I am proud to call my friends, mostly cutthroats who would gladly kill their mothers for a shell necklace. The people of the Coral Archipelago raid the nearby islands and enjoy their blood sports, while the Wavecrest Archipelago quietly tithes to the Realm and keeps the womenfolk at home while the men go to sea. And then there's Darkmist Isle and the expanding shadowland that is the Skullstone Archipelago.

In the West, I see people who guard themselves well enough against the occasional siren or group of Fair Folk who arrive riding sharks and sea horses but cannot stand against the might of the Deathlords, or against the Realm, once a new ruler sits upon the Scarlet Throne. We Westerners value our freedom, but I wonder how many of us would be willing to die for it or, more important perhaps, give up a little of that freedom in exchange for safety and unity? I think the time is coming when we will find out the answers, though they may not be the ones we want or expect.

Armattan

The South

Our duty as the Chosen of the Unconquered Sun is to bring justice and righteousness to the people, and the cities of the South are places in dire need of our guidance. They are ruled either by bandits clothed in noble trappings and finery or by despots who support their rule through magic and the artifacts of the First Age. The rulers of the South have little interest in justice, only in maintaining their rule against anything that may threaten it. They support the Realm so long as it suits them, but they are loyal to no one but themselves.

When I was first Exalted, I walked out of the desert and into the Lap because it was the safest place I could think of for me to consider my future. The more I considered it, the more I realized that the cities of the South are places of great danger to our kind. It is in the cities where the Wyld Hunt seeks us and in the cities where the rulers and their followers either seek to use us for their own ends or turn us over to the hounds of the Realm. Outside the cities, in the vast stretches between them and the deep desert of the South, our enemies cannot reach us so easily. Before I was Exalted, I would not have tried to live alone in the desert, but now, I know that I can travel through it for days without concern for food or water and without being burned by the sun. And I am never truly alone with Sirah at my side.

Yet, we cannot carry out our duty by living in isolation. It would be all too tempting to leave the conflicts of the cities behind and live in the desert. However, the desert has dangers of its own. There are the Wyld places, the Fair Folk and spirits that will flay a man's flesh from his bones with the fury of a sandstorm, so they can carve the bones into flutes for their wind-songs. But we can brave the dangers of the desert and the badlands like no others, and sometimes we must, to avoid the attention of the Realm and its agents.

The Realm

Why is the Realm our enemy? Not because of anything we have chosen, but because of the choices the Dragon-Blooded have made. If the Realm were a place of justice and righteousness, I would support its rule gladly. But the disappearance of the Scarlet Empress has shown the Realm for what it truly is, a façade of beauty and harmony covering decay and decadence that goes back for centuries. The houses of the Dragon-Blooded struggle against each other for control of the Realm, and they have withdrawn their support from the Threshold to fight their own battles, neglecting their responsibilities as rulers and guides of the people.

Not all the Dragon-Blooded are corrupt, some are fierce and loyal soldiers of the Realm, but they do not understand that their loyalty is misplaced and the empire they support is crumbling. Unfortunately, it is difficult to show them the truth of this, since they do not trust us or the words of the Unconquered Sun. We are Anathema to them, although I have known some Dragon-Blooded willing to consider us useful rather than monsters to be hunted down and destroyed.

In the Lap, I met a Dragon-Blooded woman of House Sesus, named Ignea. We met in a house of pleasure where you would not expect to find any of the Exalted. She was seeking information about a particular yassal crystal, which she'd heard had turned up somewhere in the Lap. I was looking into the death Joyous Wren, of one of the women who worked in the house, who I had known in my time in the city. It seems that Joyous Wren had last held the crystal, a gift from an unwise lover and that someone else had taken it from her, along with her life.

I do not think Ignea knew what I was at first. Perhaps she took me for a mercenary or a wanderer. She warned me to stay out of her path, a warning I ignored. The involvement of the Dragon-Blooded told me this was a matter of justice requiring my attention. So I investigated further and uncovered a plot involving an outcaste of the lady's house intent on keeping the spirit within the yassal crystal from its former owner as a means of blackmail.

When Ignea and I crossed paths again, we tested each other's mettle, and I could see that she was torn between cooperating with one of the Anathema and regaining the gem. I offered my aid, for a price, and she agreed. Together, we recovered the yassal containing the spirit of Ignea's great-grandfather, a renowned sage and advisor to her house, willingly placed there to continue to guide his descendents. Most of the money she paid me went to the sister of the woman who died because of it, an innocent caught in the struggle within Ignea's family.

Ignea made it clear to me that, should we meet again, it would not necessarily be on such friendly terms, and I believe her. Still, it proves that the Dragon-Blooded are not without honor or loyalty, even if their support of the corrupt Realm must eventually bring us into conflict.

Spirits and Fair Folk

If the Dragon-Blooded are foes we can respect and perhaps even cooperate with, then the other powers of the South are allies to be wary of or forces entirely unconcerned with our struggles.

From the shore of the Inland Sea to the depths of the desert, spirits dwell in the lands of the South, and they are powers to be reckoned with. I've heard tales of the ghosts of Chiaroscuro, although I have never seen them. My experience with spirits has been in the desert and the wild lands, where the nomads and tribes worship and propitiate the little gods with gifts to fend off their anger and capricious moods. The South is a land where fire spirits are often found, and these little gods are among the most dangerous because they are given to great passion and equally great anger when they are offended.

In my journey to the Lap, I encountered many spirits of the desert, but one took me unawares, and I nearly paid for my carelessness with my life. After walking for many days through the desert, I chose one night to stop and rest at a tiny oasis I discovered. Reclining on the shore of a small, silvery pool, my back against the trunk of a palm tree, I quickly drifted off to sleep.

In my dreams, I found myself in a hall of silken veils of many colors, blowing gently in a warm breeze that brought the scent of jasmine and orange blossoms. Delicate laughter tinkled like bells in the air as I wandered among the veils, pursuing an elusive figure that darted before me, just out of sight, seen only as a shadow against the silk, her laughter floating back to me. The touch of her hands was a pleasure incomparable, and the more I pursued, the more she sped away from me, until I plunged through the cloths to embrace a form that was at once cool and warm, slick and silken. I was desperate to feel the pleasure of her touch.

Sirah's roar awakened me as the serpentine form dragged me into the pool of the oasis. Her flesh was of fine silvery scales, silken and gleaming with wetness, while her fanged jaws opened to swallow my soul. Instead, I gave her the point of my khatar. Her screams broke the spell she'd tried to weave over me, but she still pulled me into her pool, which was far deeper than I'd imagined. Her coils gathered around me, trying to crush the breath from my lungs, but my Charms relived me of the need to breathe and gave me the strength to break her grip. I escaped from her pool and quickly left the oasis behind, though I am sure she dwells there still, waiting for the next traveler to pass by.

The Fair Folk I have seen are not the terrors described in the tales, but then, I have not seen their cataphractoi, only those who choose to take form and live in our world, among men. I have seen them as jugglers and entertainers, storytellers and performers.

The house of pleasure I visited in the Lap was run by one of the Fair Folk, named Yirini. She took the form of perhaps the most beautiful woman I had ever seen. But her beauty was not of this world, it was spun out of ice, silver and tears into a shape with pale, creamy flesh, frosty hair and a smile that broke hearts. I was surprised to find one of the Fair Folk in such a place, much less owning it, but Yirini only laughed brightly and said, "We do not all take what we need from the world. Some of us understand a fair exchange, and pleasure for dreams is a good one, is it not?" She offered me the opportunity to sample the manifold pleasures of her establishment and introduced me to Joyous Wren, who made my stay in the Lap considerably more pleasant. Wren's death was part of the reason I chose to move on. Yirini mourned Wren's death as much as any at her house, so at least some of the Fair Folk do have hearts.

Other Solar Exalted

During my time in the Lap, I also met another Solar Exalted for the first time. His name was Aranor, a mercenary by trade, but also one of the Chosen of the Unconquered Sun. He belonged to the Dawn Caste rather than the Zenith, and he was a fierce and skilled fighter. He was eager to leave the Lap, and after his conflict with some agents of the Guild, I wasn't surprised. But my encounter with him taught me two things. First, that I was not alone, that part of the old legend was true and there were other castes of Solar Exalted. Second, Aranor showed me that we work well together, we compliment each other to create a harmonious whole.

So I decided to leave the Lap and begin my journey again. I had new purpose, not only to help the common people with my gifts and further the cause of justice and righteousness, but also to seek out allies, companions for my journey. There was only so much I could accomplish alone, but with a Circle of brothers and sisters gathered around me, there would be no limit to what we could do.

So, I first gathered all the information I could about the Anathema. It was difficult, since such questions are regarded with suspicion and can bring the attention of the Immaculate Order. But enough people in the Lap knew me and knew that I was trustworthy. I pieced together what I could from what I learned and the tales I recalled. Then, I made my way back to Gem, traveling with a caravan I met along the way.

My first Solar ally found me before I could find him. On my first night in Gem, he stole into my room at the inn as silent as a shadow and placed a blade against my throat. I was surprised at how young he was. It seemed he believed some of the tales of the Anathema and thought I was a danger to him, that I had come to claim his soul now that he had been changed.

Even my Charms wouldn't protect me against a slit throat, so I spoke to him in calm and soothing tones. I told him who I was and why I'd come, about my Exaltation and the words of the Unconquered Sun. Then, I told him if he was unwilling to trust me, he would have to kill me and remain alone. He spared my life, and it was then that he discovered Sirah crouched behind him, ready to leap to my aid. We both lowered our guard and began to trust each other a bit. I learned that his name was Laughing Rain and that he was of the Night Caste, his abilities nearly the opposite of my own. Where I worked in the light, he slipped through the shadows; we make a good team, he and I.

Other business brought us here to Paragon, but now I am sure that it was the hand of the Unconquered Sun that guided us, since it allowed us to find you. Your Exaltation has freed you from bondage to the Perfect, but it may not protect you if his people take you and force you to swear to him again. The Unconquered Sun has chosen you, given you a chance at freedom and the power to change the world. You would be welcome with us, if that is what you want. The only question remains is what do you wish to do?

Fire Orchid

Mortals

What is it to be mortal in a world where spirits and gods walk abroad? It is the life of a rabbit in the forest or that of a fish in the sea or that of any beast that lives with the possibility of a predator's teeth ending its life in but a moment. I know because I lived that life once.

I was born a mortal among gods, a child of the Dragon-Blooded with none of their gifts, a throwback and a failure to my gens. The Immaculates say that the Dragon-Blooded are the closest to the Immaculate Dragons, the closest to spiritual perfection. So what sin must I have committed in a previous life to be born as a mere mortal? What shame did I bring on my house? These were not questions anyone dared to ask in my presence, but they hung in the air, unspoken, all of my life, like a foul scent that can never be chased from a room.

So, I sought the soldier's life to prove myself, and there, I found camaraderie and friendship and a measure of acceptance. It is one thing to show courage with the gifts of the gods at your command and quite another to be courageous when you have nothing but sword, shield and armor standing between you and certain death. On the battlefield, I saw some of the best and worst that humanity is capable of.

But while I think any mortal who lives life unmolested by the powers in this world is lucky, I also think one who fights and lives is luckier still. Once, I saw the world only as a game of chance and skill, and I attempted to escape from it into a retirement of obscurity. Yet, when I was Exalted by the Unconquered Sun, I realized that we Exalted can change the world for humanity. We can stand on the wall between civilization and the powers that lurk outside of it and say to them "you will not pass." We can bring some safety and comfort in an uncertain world. While we stand on that wall, between the powers and mortality, we stand outside of the village and are as close to the powers that mortals fear as we are to those we protect.

I realized a long time ago it's not safe to deal with the powers of this world, and now, I find that I am one of them.

The Dragon-Blooded and the Realm

Spiritual enlightenment, that's what I learned about the Dragon-Blooded from my earliest years, that they were close to spiritual perfection, blessed by the gifts of the Elemental Dragons. Who would not want such a blessing? It all seemed so simple then, so clear that the Dragon-Blooded were meant to rule, to guide the common folk and to protect them against threats such as the Fair Folk and the Anathema. I idolized the champions and heroes of the legions, and I loved to hear tales from the Immaculate Texts, legends of how the Chosen of the Elemental Dragons kept the world safe.

It is a difficult thing to realize what you learned as a child isn't entirely true. As I grew older and discovered that I did not partake of the glorious heritage of the Dragons, I tried to hide my shame and disappointment in casual nonchalance. I grew bitter about the power of the Dragon-Blooded, and I began to see their flaws in the light of my jealousy, looking for ways to bring them down to the level of mere mortals I had been consigned to.

I found more than a few faults there. The Scarlet Houses schemed against each other, even in those days before the Empress vanished. They maneuvered for position and favor, arranged alliances and betrayals to suit their goals. They lived in luxury, even decadence. A far cry from the vision of "spiritual perfection" I'd had as a child. My brothers, Kalim and Vosa, were inheritors of the Dragons' power, but they were also boys, as petty and cruel, and as foolish and kind, as boys can be. So were their friends, and mine, from the legion and the houses alike.

As a soldier, I saw many Dragon-Blooded officers fight with valor and daring, and I saw others abuse their positions and the trust of their troops. I knew some who would willingly die for the legion and the people of the Scavenger Lands and others who'd sacrifice a hundred lives to spare their own. The Dragon-Blooded were gifted in the arts of war, towering in their passions and in their faults, but they were no more perfect than any being in Creation.

Since the Unconquered Sun opened my eyes and my heart, I see the Terrestrial Exalted for what they are. They are heroes and villains, fathers, mothers, children, leaders, followers, all the many diverse things people can be. But the Dragon-Blooded are also a people that have lost their way in the world. They cloak themselves with pretensions of "spiritual enlightenment" they haven't earned and can't live up to. They struggle to control an empire that is not rightfully theirs. Their gifts are wasted on struggle and self-aggrandizement, climbing a mountain so they can behold their own reflections and pronounce perfect a world that was never their doing.

They should not be our enemies, they should be our allies, but fate has not made it so. I hope that we can show them the truth and work together again as the gods intended, but family or no, I will remain true to my purpose, whatever the cost.

The Fair Folk

When I was a child, I was fascinated by my mother's power over fire. She could cause flames to leap from her mouth or her hands, making them dance and spin through the air in a way that delighted me. Mother always tried to keep me safe, but it didn't take me long to burn myself and learn to respect fire as well as admire it.

"You must be careful, little flower," my mother said to me as she soothed the hurt. "Fire is beautiful but also dangerous, like many things in this world." When I first saw the Fair Folk, I thought of my mother's words: *beautiful, but also dangerous*. That is the nature of those from beyond the borders of Creation.

The Fair Folk are like fire, bright, warm and dazzling, but get too close, and you are certain to be burned — and what they embrace is quickly reduced to cold gray ash, consumed to feed their flames. I've seen the husks that Fair Folk leave behind, the people's dreams ripped from their souls. They're more dead than alive, little different from the revenants and zombies of the shadowlands — even worse since they still live, a kind of living death. I've seen other things done by troupes of Fair Folk in the Threshold, people killed like a cruel boy might kill a bug, torn limb from limb or impaled on crystal spikes just to watch their death agonies or the patterns their blood forms when it pours onto the ground.

Always there is the one neophyte soldier who asks, "Why not negotiate, build a treaty of peace between our two peoples?" I was that naïve once. But how do you negotiate with fire, especially a fire that is burning your house down around you? The Fair Folk obey rules, just as fire does, but allow a fire to escape the confines of hearth and forge, and it will devour you just as readily as it helped you. So it is with the Fair Folk. Individually, they can be as helpful as a candle or a cook-fire, as charming and beautiful as the dancing flames my mother conjured, or they can be as a searing iron or a flaming arrow. But together, they are an inferno like the Elemental Pole of Fire itself, which no one and nothing can hope to approach without being singed.

They should be treated with respect and courtesy whenever possible and handled with care. When they rage out of control, they must be doused to keep them from consuming everything in their path, and iron is as water to their flame.

The Wyld

The Fair Folk come from the Wyld, the unformed madness beyond Creation. I call it madness only because that is how we see it. It's the only way we can see a place with no rules, no substance, no *place* to it at all. But the Wyld isn't madness, it isn't anything, or perhaps, it would be more accurate to say that the Wyld is *everything*, everything that does not, and could not, exist in Creation.

The Wyld is like a hungry fire and Creation a map that curls and blackens at the edges. Sometimes fire burns a hole in the middle of the map, creating the soft places and Wyld lands that have existed since the Fair Folk stormed the gates. But by our very existence, we keep the "map" that is the world cool and damp and protect it from the "fire" of the Wyld. That is why the deaths of so many in the Great Contagion allowed the Wyld to flood into the world.

Allowed the opportunity, the Wyld would unmake everything that is, and Creation would cease to be. Everything would be a part of the Wyld, unformed nothingness and chaos. It seems that the Fair Folk want to overrun Creation and bring this about, but I've heard that some of them actually flee the Wyld and seek shelter in the stability of Creation, while others simply find their sport here. The Fair Folk that value Creation are in the minority, and many are still terrible threats, albeit for different reasons.

The other danger from the Wyld comes in the form of the barbarian tribes and the Lunar Exalted that sometimes rule them. How the Lunars existed for so long in the Wyld without going completely mad is a mystery to me. Perhaps they *are* completely mad; after all, they launch attacks on the outskirts of Creation for no apparent reason. Yet, I've heard other Solars tell tales of meeting Lunars that did them no harm, although they were as skittish as wild beasts. Whatever the Lunar Exalted may have been, time in the Wyld has changed them.

Wind

Mortals

Gentle Song,

I scarcely know how to begin this letter. I don't even know if you will ever see it, though I'm told that it will seem to be an innocuous collection of stories and legends to anyone else who reads it. I hope that you do read it and consider what I have to say.

I am sorry for the way we parted that night in Gethamane but not sorry that I helped to save you, and I ask you to remember that. I helped to save your life, and so did Raiton. Whatever you have been told about us, we are not monsters, we are not the Anathema the Perfected Masters speak of. In my heart, I am the same Wind you knew and befriended, but my eyes have been opened to greater truths.

The people of the world are a part of the Incarnas' plans for Creation. Not just as souls working their way toward perfection, but as souls living in this place and time. This life matters as much as in the next life and the one after that, and I believe its not just spiritual lessons we're here to learn, we're here to learn how to live and to be.

Long ago, the gods chose people and granted them the power to fight against the enemies of the gods, to cast those out of Creation. The gods empowered the Exalted to guard the world from danger, to rule wisely and well. But what the legends and the sutras don't talk about, in singing the praises of the Elemental Dragons and their children, is that the gods made the Exalted for a reason, the same reason I was chosen that night. The gods made us to protect *you*, Gentle Song. They made us to protect and help the people of the world.

That's why I can't just turn my back on you, why I wanted to try and help you understand what's become of me. Because I believe that you matter, just like your family and mine and all the folk who live in the world without feeling the weight of the gods' favor on their shoulders. I wish it was as easy as telling you what I've learned, but as a friend of mine has said, "The truth is the sharpest sword, and sometimes, you have to cut in order to heal, in order to change."

In the time to come, you may hear stories about me, and some of them will sound terrible. Know that I do what I must for the world and for the people in it.

The Dragon-Blooded

Kirin,

My friend, I hope that I don't endanger you with this letter or with our friendship because I always valued it. In our days together as students in the temple, I was awed by you, Dragon-Blooded, son of a great house. I was so honored that you even deigned to be my friend, that you took an interest in me and helped me to learn. You probably won't be surprised to know that I also envied you your gifts. I know it wasn't the way we were taught, but part of me longed for the spiritual enlightenment you knew, so near to the Immaculate Dragons.

Now, I've discovered that much of what I believed is not true, much like what you must believe about me now. The truth is, Kirin, that we both have power now, and I've tested mine against the Dragon-Blooded, as you probably already know. The gods have chosen us both, my friend, and placed our destinies before us. It's up to us to choose whether or not we will follow them. I know that my purpose in the world is to serve the Unconquered Sun and carry his message to everyone. The truth has been hidden for too long. Do you know your destiny, your purpose, Kirin?

Perhaps it's what your family and the Immaculate Order have always told you, that you're better than the common folk, nearer to spiritual perfection, and therefore, meant to rule over them in the name of the Elemental Dragons. But consider for a moment the possibility that you're wrong, that what you've been told is a lie. You know me, Kirin. Am I a monster? Am I a pawn of Malfeas? The Unconquered Sun has opened my eyes, as I hope he will open yours someday. It was never meant to be the Dragon-Blooded alone, but all Exalted, working in harmony: the Solars, the Lunars, the Sidereals, the Terrestrials and, perhaps, even the servants of the Deathlords themselves. Not just as rulers of the people, but also as servants of the gods in the name of the people.

I want you to know that I hold no malice toward you and yours. I still value our friendship, and I hope that one day I can call you my friend again. But I also know my destiny, and if it takes me to the camps of the legions or the temples of the Immaculate Order or even to the Blessed Isle itself, I won't allow anyone, friend or no, to stand in my way. There is far more at risk than a single friendship or a single life, and we are only part of a greater destiny.

The Immaculate Order

My friends, when we first came to the Palace Sublime, we believed that a higher truth brought us there, to seek spiritual enlightenment and the purification of our souls. When we began our quest to find new Immaculate Texts and artifacts of the First Age, it was, to me, an expression of our search, our need for truth to carry our souls onward to enlightenment. Looking back along the road, I see that it was a journey toward truth, but a truth none of us would have imagined then, which I must bring to you now.

The Immaculate Order is a lie.

I can already hear the gasp, the words echoing in your thoughts. Heretic! Blasphemous! You wonder if I truly am one of the Anathema. Perhaps, as the Perfected Hierarchy sees it, I am, since I carry a truth that they have labeled heresy. The truth is that we should respect the Incarna, who fought and overcame the Yozis and imprisoned them beyond the walls of the world — gods such as Gaia, who created the Elemental Dragons as her children and, through them, the Dragon-Blooded. Now the Dragon-Blooded think to Exalt themselves, when it is the gods who Exalt us. The Immaculate Order of Dragons is nothing more than a means of securing the rule of the Scarlet Houses and the Dragon-Blooded over the Realm and the whole of Creation.

The truth is even more tragic because I know first hand of the good that the Immaculate Order has done. It has helped to create peace and spread learning throughout the Realm. It is a source of serenity and purpose for thousands of people, a channel for the impulses of younger scions of the Dragons, a chance for betterment for common folk. But those things are tainted by the deception buried deep at the order's roots, which poisons all the fruits of its labors. I am sure that most of the monks and priests of the order are no more aware of the truth than I was, for they are but pawns in this game. But that does not change the fact that the truth must be brought to light, even if it means the end of the order. If I must tear away the veil of lies from each follower, priest and monk, one by one, then so be it. Even if the work takes a hundred years, it will be done.

The Lunar Exalted

Sula told me to forget my encounter with Raiton the night she took me in — and many times since then. Eventually, I simply stopped talking with her about the Lunar Exalted. I think she takes this as contentment on my part, but that isn't entirely true. Part of me still wonders about the mysterious Lunar Exalted, who was something to me in a life before this, whose Essence is still connected with mine in a way that I cannot explain and may never understand.

I've learned more about the Chosen of Luna since my first meeting with Raiton in Gethamane. How little I knew about them when I was just a monk! To the Immaculate Order, all Anathema are the same. What little information we found about the Lunars supported the belief that they were as corrupt as their brethren but that some of them fled into the Wyld after the other Anathema were overthrown. I wonder what becomes of evidence to the contrary, when researchers of the order come across it.

From what I have learned, the Lunar Exalted have suffered a great injustice, perhaps even more so than we have. But they are also not the same as the Exalted who ruled by the Solars' side so long ago. When the Dragon-Blooded rebelled, most of the Lunars fled into exile. As Lunar Exalted died and were reborn into this life, the Wyld Hunt slew them, save for those that escaped into the Wyld lands and sheltered under the wing of their elders. So, the beloved of Luna have abided in the wilderness for centuries, since the fall of the Old Realm.

I can scarcely imagine life in the Wyld for so long. I have seen the madness at the edge of Creation and what it does to the mind and the body, much less the soul. I recall the look in Raiton's eyes, his skittishness, like a trapped bird. The years have made our Lunar cousins more beast than man in many respects. Sula believes they are no longer the Exalted they once were, and I agree, but the question is, can they be again? If there is hope for the Lunar Exalted, then we owe them as great a debt as Raiton felt he owed me. If we Pillars of the Sun are to guide and teach, then we should not forget the Children of the Moon who live and howl in the Wyld. I know I will not, and one day, Raiton and I will meet again.

The Sidereal Exalted

If the Solar Exalted are fire, bright and fierce, the Lunar Exalted are water, deep, ever changing and mysterious. The Terrestrial Exalted are like wood, fertile and growing, covering the Earth, while the Sidereal Exalted, the chosen of the Five Maidens, are air. They are intellect, learning, insight and, most of all, patience.

In my time with the Cult of the Illuminated, I have come to know Sula and other Sidereals and understand more about their nature. I can hardly imagine the patience they have had to have to carry out the mission the Maidens have charged them with. I've found that you certainly need patience to deal with the Sidereal Exalted for any length of time, as well. Their riddles and lectures can sometimes make those of the masters of the Immaculate Order pale in comparison, yet they reveal a deeper, more ancient wisdom.

When I first sought shelter with the Cult of the Illuminated, I was uncertain of the destiny that was placed before me, still clinging in many ways to my former life. Sula showed great patience in teaching me. She began by answering the many questions I had about the nature of the Exalted, although there are mysteries even to the scholars of the Maidens. They do not know, for example, who will be chosen to be Exalted, although Sula says that some horoscopes do show greater potential than others and that the Sidereals can sometimes guess when and where an individual is more likely to be Exalted — but not with any reliability.

Unlike the Lunars, the surviving Sidereal Exalted still carry out the duties they were chosen for all those centuries ago. As champions of the Five Maidens, they were the advisors, sages, viziers and administrators of the Old Realm. Since the rebellion of the Dragon-Blooded, they have worked in secret, preserving ancient knowledge and preparing for the return of the Solar Exalted as was foretold to them. Sula told me of a prophecy that we would help to lead the world back to the greatness it knew in the First Age. Toward that end, the Cult of the Illuminated secretly gathers any Solar Exalted it finds, to hide them from the hunters of the Realm. It's only recently that they've been able to find and save more than a tiny handful of us.

I am grateful to the Sidereals, particularly Sula, for their help, although, at times, I wish I shared their patience. I know there are things they haven't told me yet, that they feel I'm not ready for, and that is frustrating. They also prefer to work slowly and cautiously, while, every day, I feel the need to do something more. The time of the prophecy is at hand, and soon, the time for waiting will be over.

Secrets of the Sidereals

Some of the things the Sidereal Exalted have not told Wind (or the other Solar Exalted involved with the Cult of the Illuminated) include truths that might turn the Solars against their Sidereal mentors and allies.

The Sidereals play down many of their powers to the Solars. For example, they are fully capable of predicting Celestial Exaltations by studying the stars and planets. Many of the "chance" and "fortunate" meetings with newly Exalted Solars have been carefully planned and arranged. The Sidereals are also masters of crafting prophecies to suit their own ends. The doctrines of the Cult of the Illuminated are full of such "holy sutras" and "ancient prophecies," interpreted to suit the cult's true masters.

Of course, the Gold faction that controls the Cult of the Illuminated also carefully hides the key role that the Sidereal Exalted played in the downfall of the Solars at the end of the First Age.

Chapter Four
Voices Not Our Own

The members of the Zenith Caste were the first of the returned Solar Exalted to gain the world's attention, appearing out of the wilderness bearing the words of the Unconquered Sun. At first, many dismissed them as hermits or madmen, but events since have shown that they are what they claim to be, and proof of their divine mission has begun to shake the foundations of the world. The role of the Pillars of the Sun as leaders and guides is well known to many, who either fear the possibility of uprisings created by the Solar Exalted or else look to the incarnate gods walking the Earth for hope and guidance in these dark times.

Mortals

The reaction of mortals encountering the Hammers of Heaven can be summed up in one word: awe. More than any of the Solar Exalted, the Zeniths inspire awe in those who see them. Few mortals meet one of the Zeniths and go away from it unchanged.

In lands dominated by the philosophy of the Immaculate Order, the Solar Exalted are still considered Anathema, and the Zeniths are the Blasphemous, the worst of all, who corrupt the good and decent and force them to worship at the bloody altars of their forbidden gods.

The Zeniths were the first of the Solar Exalted to return, and their renewed presence has begun to wear away at the Immaculate claim that the Celestial Exalted are Anathema. Some people have been shown the truth of the Zeniths' nature and purpose. But many still believe what they have been told all their lives and recall stories of the terrible acts of the Blasphemous before the Dragon-Blooded overthrew them. A Zenith Exalted with a reputation who enters a strange village for the first time may be met by throngs of eager new followers, a collection of wary skeptics or a lynch mob, and he can never be sure which it will be.

Since they are so few in number, the Solar Exalted often conceal their true nature, but the Zenith Caste is the least likely to do so. The Resplendent Suns' purpose is to lead and inspire, and they cannot do so by hiding their light beneath a bushel. How will the truth about the Solars' return ever be known unless the Exalted are allowed to tell it? So, the Zeniths are often the most visible of all the Solar Exalted. Tales are spreading of their appearance throughout Creation, calling for people to follow them and cast off the yoke of the Realm, teaching and helping to guide others toward righteousness and punishing the guilty with the full fury of Heaven.

More than any other Solar Exalted, the Zeniths draw fervent followers to them like a flame draws moths. People see the power of the Resplendent Suns and realize the power and majesty of the old gods. They beg the Zeniths for their blessings and their protection against the powers abroad in the world, from the hungry ghosts that prowl the shadowlands to the small gods of the wilderness, from the unleashed forces of the Wyld to the Fair Folk. "Protect us! Save us!" cry the people, and the Pillars of the Sun answer their prayers. Such deeds create more loyalty and goodwill than centuries of the Immaculate Order's teachings and philosophy. Still, the Pillars of the Sun do understand the need to move cautiously in these dangerous times and accept the guidance of their more subtle Night and Twilight brethren in some matters.

There are few rulers, in the Threshold or in the Realm, who do not feel a touch of concern when the stories of the Zenith Caste reach their ears. The power of the Solar Thunders to sway the people to their cause and to unite unruly mobs into a powerful army at their back causes more than a few despots and nobles to suffer sleepless nights. There are some who believe they can control these upstarts and others who think that no rabble-rouser can challenge them, but most look at the influence of the Zeniths with concern, envy and no small amount of fear. While rulers may countenance other Solar Exalted in their domains, even find ways to employ them toward their own ends, the Zenith Caste Solars represent a threat to their rule, even when they claim otherwise. The Resplendent Suns once ruled all of Creation. Who is foolish enough to believe that they do not plan to do so again some day?

The common folk, on the other hand, often see the Zenith Exalted as saviors, liberators that lead people to overthrow the despots and tyrants who have ruled them for so long. Stories spread in secret about their powers and their deeds and about how they were betrayed by the Dragon-Blooded but have returned to reclaim the Realm and save the world from falling into darkness and madness. Witnesses to the deeds of the Resplendent Suns are among their most fervent converts, gathering to follow the Zeniths to the ends of Creation or helping to spread the message they carry, that the time of despair is over, that the champions of the Unconquered Sun have returned.

Masi of Rana

Yes, I have the honor of knowing Madame General Karal Fire Orchid, who saved us all from the rampage of the Fair Folk and helped to protect us in our time of need. She is, by far, the most majestic and beautiful lady in all Creation. Her wisdom is without equal, and her sword raised against her enemies is invincible.

For a time, she lived among us as any other lady of means might do, but even then, I saw something great about her. I heard that she was a soldier for many years and that she commanded the loyalty of many men. She was very humble and didn't like to talk about her exploits in battle, although she did indulge me from time to time and told stories about how she fought in this part of the Threshold or another, against the enemies of Lookshy. She always said that a soldier's life was difficult but important.

After she saved me from the riders of the Fair Folk, Madame Fire Orchid was different. She stood straighter and taller than I had seen before, and her eyes flashed with a commanding spirit that could not be ignored. Wearing her red enameled armor and wielding her flashing sword, she drove off the Fair Folk. They feared her power, as any thinking creature should. I saw her kill two of them as easily as you or I might dispatch rabbits. With two swipes of her sword, she cut through armor and flesh as easily as grass.

In the days that followed, Madame Fire Orchid taught us the arts of war. Although her prowess in battle was remarkable, her wisdom as a leader was even greater. From her, we learned how to protect ourselves against attack and to fortify Rana for when the Fair Folk or any other danger threatens. When the time comes, I will fight for my village, as our glorious hero taught me, and I will fight anyone who dares to say that the Chosen of the Unconquered Sun such as Madame Fire Orchid are Anathema. We have seen the truth for ourselves.

Gentle Song

Oh, Wise, Perfect and Immaculate Dragons, hear my unworthy prayer. My heart is filled with doubt, fear and longing, and I come to you seeking wisdom and peace. Since that night in Gethamane, I have known none.

I am plagued by nightmares where I relive that night over and over again. The nameless thing that creeps into my chamber, smelling of decay and a sickly sweet, overripe scent. Its loathsome touch on my skin. The sound of my screams in the night, bringing help in the form of Wind, glowing like a fallen star from Heaven, fighting alongside Kirin and the black-cloaked stranger to save me. Oh, the glory of that light shining around Wind! The gratitude I felt for his bravery and valor! Then comes the disappointment, the growing realization, the fear, when I began to understand what had happened. The look in Wind's eyes, so confused and forlorn, as he turned to the window and followed the black-cloaked figure out into the night, a star falling into the darkness.

Kirin was reluctant to speak out against Wind, and I think because he wants to protect me, but I am not a child. I have studied the Immaculate Texts even more than he has, and I know the truth of what happened that night, although I still cannot bring myself to believe it in my heart. Like me, Wind received a visitor in the night, but his wore the form of the youth in black, with skin as pale as the moon. But there was no one to save Wind from the peril he faced. I know now that his visitor was one of the Anathema, who ruled the world once long ago, and that he tempted Wind with his wiles and his promises of power.

What passed between them, I do not know. Did Wind deny him at first? I like to think that he did, that he realized some of the danger to his soul. But when he heard my cries of terror, what passed through Wind's mind and heart? Oh, Immaculate Masters, let him not have succumbed out of fear for me! But he said in his letter that he took up this burden, that he was chosen, to protect me. The wiles of the Anathema are great and terrible! Wind seems certain that he is the Chosen of the gods, a champion of the people, when he is being deceived, led astray by the Anathema who have corrupted him.

Forgive my weakness, oh, Immaculate Dragons, but I cannot give Wind's letter to my masters, although I fear for him greatly. I will allow the smoke from this fire to carry it to Heaven, and I ask that you watch over and protect him. If it is your will, free him from the fate that has befallen him. If he suffers it because of me, then let his doom fall upon me instead, so that he may be safe!

Tanar

I've been at sea for most of my life, but never have I seen anything like the courage and power of my captain, Ocean Pearl. She brought down Blackheart, the Man Who Could Not Die and liberated the *Scarlet Saber*. She saved us all then, and she has since saved my life more times than I can count. Any man, beast or spirit that threatens her will have to deal with me first. I would gladly give my life for her, and I know that goes for any member of this crew.

There are times when Ocean Pearl chooses to take me into her confidence, when we sit in her cabin or stand at the wheel of the *Saber* and talk about things, and I'm honored that she considers me a confidant. One day, while we were sailing on the open waters, the sky an endless blue above, the sun shining warmly on our faces, I asked her a question I'd long wondered about.

"What is it like to be one of the Exalted?" I said.

Ocean Pearl looked at me curiously and thoughtfully for a moment, then she gave me a smile that could lighten men's hearts and break them in the same moment and laughed.

"It's difficult to describe," she said. "It's as if, in a moment, everything in the world becomes *more*. You feel stronger, faster, braver, more cunning than before. The sights and sounds seem more alive, time seems to slow. Other things become greater, too: your duties, your choices, your enemies, but there's always guidance to turn to," she said, looking up at the shining face of the sun and smiling again.

What she said is true, at least from my point of view. Ocean Pearl is a goddess of grace and skill, a leader without equal, but she is also still a woman. She is loyal to her friends and crew, fierce to her enemies. She has her doubts and even fears, but when the time comes, she always overcomes them to do what she feels is right, and that, I think, is her most important quality. Some men say that it would be easy to be courageous if they had the power of the Exalted at their command, but Ocean Pearl was ready to fight Blackheart even before she was chosen. I think the Exalted are chosen for their great courage. Theirs is a great power but also a heavy burden, so the Unconquered Sun knows to choose well. He certainly did so with my captain.

Burning Wind

A demon, I tell you! No, one of the Anathema themselves! I am certain of it. We fell upon a caravan in the desert as our lord the Perfect of Paragon commanded us, for we can do no other than his will. I saw this man fall underneath the blade of my brother, but he rose from the dead, like some revenant, only he was not dead.

He came into our camp all aflame, in the company of wild lions hungry for the flesh of men. His blade cut through our ranks as if ripping through silk, blood soaking the sands red. Three men fell dead at once, cut to pieces before we even overcame the shock of his appearance. He roared in a fearsome voice that shook the sands and turned my heart to ice in my chest. I am not ashamed to say that I fled from that terrible sight as fast as my legs could carry me. Behind, I could hear only the shouts and pleas of the dying as he butchered my brothers like cattle.

Only a handful of us escaped from the monster, alone in the desert without mounts or supplies. We traveled all night and into the day before we sought shelter from the sun and collapsed into a fevered sleep. But the next night, when we set off again, there came a great roaring across the dunes, the sound of a hunting lion. Broken Opal nearly lost his wits crying out in terror until we cuffed him into silence. Little good it did us because soon the Blasphemous was upon us again.

Yes, I am sure now it could only have been one of the most unholy and corrupt of the Anathema. For 10 nights and days, he has hunted us through the desert, giving us no rest and no mercy. I am the last of all my brothers, the only one to survive his hunt and reach shelter. I beg you, kind folk, for the shade and water of your camp, for rest and comfort. No, please! Do not turn away! I am at your mercy! The sun is sinking, and the hunter will come for me! Please! Have mercy! Oh, Perfect, protect me!

Other Solar Exalted

The Pillars of the Sun are well named, since they are often the solid center around which a Circle of Solar Exalted orbits. In the First Age, the Zeniths were the leaders of the Solar Exalted, guiding their brothers and sisters with their wisdom and keeping them on the path of righteousness. The Resplendent Suns continue many of those responsibilities in the Second Age, carrying the message of the Unconquered Sun and encouraging their fellow Solars to take up his cause of righteousness in the world.

Unfortunately, not all Solars are so eager to follow the guidance of the Zenith Caste, particularly when it brings them into conflict with the Realm and many of the other great powers of the world. Many would rather conceal their true nature in order to avoid the Wyld Hunt and other dangers, while some have their own agendas that don't necessarily involve taking lessons in morals from strangers. It can take some effort for one of the Resplendent Suns to convince these Solar Exalted to do the right thing (sometimes backed up with a more direct physical argument).

Generally, the Zenith Caste is well regarded by its fellow Solars. The Pillars of the Sun represent the best and brightest, the things that are good about the Solar Exalted and humanity. Some of the other castes (particularly the Night Caste) are keenly aware that it is their duty to handle some of the "dirty work" so that the Zeniths can keep their eyes focused on the Heavens and their ideals.

Swan

You want to know why Panther and Dace are going to Rubylak to convince the Linowan to help us and not me? That's simple, it's what Panther does best, and a wise man knows to stick to what he does best and let other people do what they do best rather than trying to take everything upon himself. I'm a diplomat and a negotiator. That made me the natural choice to go to Thorns and arrange an agreement with the Deathlord. I know that Panther wouldn't have fared at all well there. He probably would have tried to pull the Deathlord's palace down around him; my brother is not particularly tolerant of the Deathlords or their agents.

But that's to be expected; Panther, he isn't a diplomat. He's a leader, and there's a difference. He doesn't believe in carefully chosen words or even polite lies for the sake of smoothing things out. He doesn't bargain, and he doesn't haggle (trust me, I've wandered through more than a few marketplaces with him). What he does know how to do is to think and to act honorably, to know what the right thing is and then do it. He can inspire a crowd and make them realize the importance of things they may have overlooked — or just choose not to see. The Linowan respond far better to someone who seems forthright and honorable than, well, to put it bluntly, a diplomat who could just as easily be a spy. They've see too many Haltan "diplomats" like that, I'm sure.

Panther will make the Queen understand our concerns, if anyone can. I've seen him in some difficult situations, and he never gives up or backs down. You can always depend on him to keep going no matter what. When we begin to tire or feel overwhelmed by the task before us, Panther is always the one who helps us to pick up and keep moving forward. He's sometimes a bit too blunt and honest — I don't think he always wants to know how Harmonious Jade and I get things done — but when it comes to having a solid, dependable center to our Circle, I couldn't ask for anyone better.

Laughing Rain

When I was a boy, I used to love listening to the sound of the rain. My mother told me it was because it was raining so hard the night I was born and she heard the rain chuckling and laughing along the roof — that's how I got my name. I'd listen to the crash of the thunder and watch the flashes of lightning through the window, thinking of the battles being fought between the sky spirits up among the clouds. When I imagined the voices of the thunder spirits, they sounded a lot like Armattan. His voice can crack like thunder, and I haven't seen many who can stand up to it.

My Zenith brother is a lot like lightning. Blazing bright, he strikes instantly with power and precision. In Armattan, there's little doubt, no time to weigh a decision. He sees what needs to be done, and he does it. Of course, I've done what I can to teach him the value of prudence and stealth, but he usually leaves those things to me, just like I leave the decision-making to him. He knows what to do in most situations, and although his choices aren't always the easiest ones (in fact, they rarely ever are), I can at least say that life with him is never dull!

It can be easy to think that Zeniths such as Armattan are solely concerned with meting out justice and upholding their moral code to the exclusion of all else, but that's just not true. Armattan is a man of great mercy, when it's called for. When we first met, I stole into his room at the Inn of Quiet Repose in Gem, thinking he was a monster I had to slay. He could have had his lion kill me then and there, but he saw that I was confused and frightened, and he helped me instead. He cares very much about the suffering and needs of others. That's why he feels so driven to help and see that they get justice. I've seen him carry injured folk for miles without resting and go without food or drink so that he can give what he has to those in need.

His endurance and, most of all, his patience, are remarkable. I can slip past any sentry, but Armattan can crouch down in the sand or the grass and sit there motionless for hours on end, silently waiting for something to happen. He must be patient — he put up with me when we first met and took the time to overcome my fears and earn my trust. When he takes on a task, he follows it to the very end, no matter how long it takes. That's why I think we're both fortunate, you and I, and why I think the Perfect of Paragon should start sleeping lightly at night. Armattan doesn't forget, and he doesn't rest until justice is done.

Demetheus

I haven't met a lot of other Solars, but of the ones I have met, the "Zenith Caste" have got to be the worst. Not that they're bad people, just that I don't see things the way they do, and if anything bothers one of them, it's meeting up with someone they can't get to see things their way, especially another Solar. You see, the Zeniths are all about getting people together to do things their way. They see themselves as priests and prophets of the Unconquered Sun, so they figure that they ought to be in charge, right? Sorry, but that's not part of the deal as far as I'm concerned. I do things my own way. I don't need a holier-than-thou priest looking over my shoulder all the time telling me which way the wind blows.

Worse than that, most of the Zenith Caste usually already have people following them around who are convinced that they've got some special insight into the way things work. These cults of followers trail along behind them like puppies yapping at their heels. Not the best way to keep a low profile where the Dragon-Blooded are concerned, if you ask me.

That's the other thing about them that kind of bothers me. It's the way that, no matter how hard you try, there's just something so damn *admirable* about the Zeniths. There's something that makes you want to listen to what they have to say, and before you know it, you're nodding along like they're making perfect sense even when they're talking about the most lame-brained ideas you've ever heard. There's something just not right about the way they can give a little speech and have an entire crowd in the palm of their hand.

Me, I don't believe in speeches. If a man has a problem with me, he can say it straight to my face. If I don't like what he has to say, he's going to lose a few teeth. If he can beat me fair and square, good for him, although I haven't met the man yet who can take me in a fight. Forget about all of the speeches and the grand plans and the preaching. I leave that to the Zeniths. They seem to enjoy it, and gods know, they're good at it.

The Dragon-Blooded

Who among the Terrestrial Exalted do not feel some touch of concern, even fear, at the mention of the Resplendent Suns, the Hammers of Heaven, returned to the world to carry out the will of the Unconquered Sun and, perhaps, seek justice for the wrongs done to them so long ago? Of course, few of the Dragon-Blooded know the truth about the fall of the Solar Exalted. Many scions of the Realm firmly believe the tenets of the Immaculate Philosophy and hold fast to the idea that their ancestors rebelled and overthrew the Anathema, terrible overlords. To them, the returning Solars are mythic monsters come to life to challenge their rightful rule and the natural order of the world.

Kirin, speaking with Master Sulin

"Master, I do not understand, what has become of Wind? Why are we not searching for him even now? He may be in great danger, I—"

"I know that you are brave, Kirin, and your loyalty to your friend does you credit, but there is nothing that we can do for Wind now. His fate is in the hands of the Immaculate Dragons and the Wyld Hunt."

"The Wyld Hunt? But, Master, surely...."

"You have told me what you saw, Kirin, and so has Gentle Song. There can be no question. Wind has been taken by one of the Anathema and may have joined their ranks himself this night."

"No! I can't believe that of Wind! He would never do such a thing."

"He may not have had any choice, young one. The temptations and wiles of the Anathema are a thousand-fold. They can influence a man's heart and mind. Did you not say that Wind ran away moments after the first body was found in the alley? Perhaps the Anathema touched him even then. Perhaps he knew of its presence before then."

"I am sure that he did not, Master."

"Are you? And how are you so certain of this, Kirin?"

"Wind is my friend. I know him, Master. I trust him."

"I see, and how do you explain what has happened?"

"I... I cannot."

"Perhaps you should consider your own role in this, Kirin, and what you will say before the other masters of the temple when we return. Remember, the wiles of the Anathema are many, and they taint whatever they touch."

From a Letter to Wind

My friend,

I was pleased and grateful to receive your letter. It may be hard to believe, but I am. Not the response you expected, is it? It's been a long while since we've seen each other, Wind, and you're right, I've heard stories of things from the Threshold. I've started to learn that you can't believe everything you hear, only what you see and what you know in your heart is true.

One of those things is that you are my friend, Wind, and I have always been yours. You are more of a brother to me than any brother of the blood could be. Since that night in Gethamane, a shadow has fallen over us all. I've found my duties at the temple limited, and both Gentle Song and I have been kept here, where we can be watched and questioned. The questioning stopped some time ago, when they finally realized we knew nothing of what happened to you, but things have never been the same since. We're no longer trusted. Our association with you, one of the Anathema, taints us.

Even as I write it, I cannot believe it. Master Sulin says the Anathema have many tricks and wiles to deceive us, but I know you, Wind, and I fought alongside you to kill the creature that menaced Gentle Song. If you were some Anathema, why flee? Why help protect Gentle Song at all?

I find it just as hard to believe what you say about the Immaculate Order. I am torn between loyalty to my friend and to the order that has given purpose to my life. Still, you risked all to contact me and tell me what you knew, while the order has kept me here, watched me and treated me like *I* am Anathema.

You said that you know the truth, and I want to know it. I still value our friendship, too, and I want to prove that to you. I want you to meet me in the Threshold. I have a way of getting to the North, if you'll agree to meet me there this summer. I swear on all that I hold sacred that this isn't a trick or a trap and that I will come alone. All that I ask in return is that you promise me the protection of my friend and the truth as you know it. I'm entrusting this letter to a friend of my family. His discretion can be relied upon. I hope to hear from you soon.

Your friend,

Kirin

Gens Karal

"Another town in the Scavenger Lands protected against attack by the 'Warrior Clad in Red Steel and Fire,' and another town lost to the Anathema." Karal Kalim said flatly, tossing the missive he was reading down onto a table already heavy with maps and other papers, most of them decorated with the stamp of the Seventh Legion's intelligence directorate.

"I have said, do not use that word in reference to your sister, Kalim!" Karal Linwei said hotly, turning to look at her eldest son.

"But mother—" Vosa began from where he sat by the table.

"No!" General Linwei said, cutting him off with a chop of her hand. The scion of the Karal gens had a commanding presence her sons had learned to respect. "I will *not* hear Fire Orchid spoken of in that manner, do you understand? There is no proof...."

"Mother," Vosa began again patiently. "There is ample proof. You simply don't want to see it." When Linwei turned a withering glare on him, Vosa steeled himself not to shrink from it. Although it pained him — pained them all — he *had* to get his mother to see the truth. "There's no mistaking the descriptions," he continued. "In Mela's blessed name, she's used her true name through much of it! And the tales they tell in Rana of her—"

"I still will not believe that your sister is one of the Anathema!" Linwei stormed. "And if she is, then the stories of the Anathema are lies! I know my own daughter!"

"Whether it is true or not, mother," Kalim said, rallying to his brother's side, "it doesn't matter if we believe it, it only matters if the other officers believe it. People are becoming concerned with these emergent Anathema or whatever they are. Our enemies have heard the same tales that we have, and you *know* that they will try to use them against us! If we don't get concrete information, we can expect to see this turned against us in the General Staff meetings." He let that possibility hang in the air for a moment, rather than further stoke his mother's anger. "Either way, we must know the truth and settle this threat to our family's honor."

The passion and energy that animated Karal Linwei seemed to leave her in a rush as she sighed and smoke poured from her mouth and nostrils. The ruddy glow of her skin dampened, and she suddenly looked almost every day of her hundred-some years.

"You're right, both of you," she said to her sons, nodding her head sadly. "We must uncover the truth of this, for the sake of the family and our future in Lookshy, and your sister must either be exonerated, or her memory must be avenged." She left unspoken the possibility that it might mean the two brothers having to hunt down a mad god that was once their sister.

"Then, we may go, mother?" Kalim asked, and Linwei nodded in support.

"Yes. Go, and learn what you can, before the Wyld Hunt gets too close. Take a detachment of helots with you. There are some reliable men in the ranger unit of the field force on garrison duty. I'll see to it that you receive a talon of their best men as escorts."

Vosa stood and moved over to Kalim's side of the table, both men offering their mother a deep and respectful bow.

"And be careful," Linwei said to them gently as they turned to leave. "I may have already lost a daughter. I do not want to lose my sons as well."

The Lunar Exalted

The signs and portents of the return of the Solar Exalted have reached even the edges of the Wyld, the hidden places where the Lunar Exalted have lurked for so long on the fringes of Creation. The wise Children of Luna have seen and heard evidence that their Solar brethren have returned to the world, and they find their hearts filled with conflicting feelings about this news.

Once, the Lunars and the Solars served the gods and ruled the whole of Creation together. They were balanced in perfect harmony, with the Lunars often taking Solars as their mates and consorts. But they say that love is blind, and love blinded the Lunars to the failings of their mates and the growing power of the curse placed on the Solar Exalted. Only at the end, when the Dragon-Blooded rebelled, did the Lunars acquiesce and permit usurpation. Embittered, the Lunar Exalted fled into the Wyld reaches at the edge of the world.

It has been a long time since the Lunar Exalted have had any place in civilization, and they have rejected the world that rejected them. They have been betrayed many times: by the corruption that grew within the Solar Exalted, by the Sidereal Exalted, who engineered the Lunar fall and by the Dragon-Blooded, who carried out the coup. Some Lunars are hateful of the civilization that produced such duplicity and seek to destroy the milieu that brought about their shame, while others are less bitter but no more forgiving and shun the world of men. The world of beasts is simpler and knows no betrayal.

But now, the light of their Solar counterparts has returned to the world, and some Lunars are drawn from their dark caves and lairs to see it again. The return of the Zenith Caste heralded the return of the Solar Exalted, and many Lunars are uncertain how to feel. Some are drawn to the Solars' light, longing to feel its warmth again, even for a moment. These Lunars try to right ancient wrongs and to atone for their sins of long ago. But others still feel the pain of ancient betrayal and wish to punish the inheritors of the Solar mantle for it. Some Lunars have dwelt in the Wyld so long they have forgotten any sort of human life. It remains to be seen if the Resplendent Suns can coax the Lunar Exalted from their strongholds and ignite compassion and understanding in their hearts or if the Solars will be forced to fight against their former allies, their former friends and mates.

Raiton

It's true, sister, what they say. The Solar Exalted have returned to the world. I saw one reborn before my eyes, as the dreams and visions guided me. How long since I last basked in that golden warmth? How long since that light guided us all and inspired us to greatness? It's hard to tell sometimes, just how long it has been, and the world is a different place than it was in those days. I was happy then, soaring among the vast towers of the Realm, flying across the length and breadth of the land, seeing what there was to be seen and bringing my visions back to the tower where my beloved waited to hear about them all. I thought that nothing could escape my notice then, but some things did, and they were the downfall of us all.

He's so bright, this new Zenith, like the sun on a clear, cold day in the North, when the air is as pure as crystal and the light shines off the snow. He's so different from what I remember, and yet, the light… the light is the same as always. The Unconquered Sun has chosen him — and others. He has turned his attention back to Creation now that the children of the Elemental Dragons squabble and fight among themselves. But there is still danger for the Chosen of the Unconquered Sun — and for us. The Wyld Hunt still stalks the land. I guided him away from them, helped him to get away. I owed him at least that much for my betrayal then. A part of me wanted to stay behind, to protect him, to help teach him, but I don't think I can be again what I was before. I've changed too much — the world has changed too much — for it to be just like it was before. Will I see him again? I think that I will, though I cannot say where or how or what we will do then.

What does the return of the Solars mean for us, sister? What can the Solar Thunders do but raise their voices and shine their light in the darkness, asking others to follow where they lead. Will we follow? I don't know that I would. The Solars died, but we were the ones who suffered. While they slept in their prison of jade, we lost all that we had, fled into the Wyld, did what we had to do to survive alone without that pure and guiding light. Do we really need the Solars any longer? Haven't we survived without them for more than 1,000 years? Where were they when we struggled in the Wyld? Where were they when I had the first markings cut into my flesh to hold it there when it shifted and flowed like water? Yes, yes, they were dead, I know, because we failed them. Now, they are returning, and I feel the draw of their light and warmth. It's easier not to think about such things.

Luna taught us that change is the way of the world, the only constant. We must change, or we will die. What change is coming, sister, and will I change with it or die this time? Death may be the better change, there are times when I longed for it, but I don't think I'm ready to join you in death just yet. The light has come back into the world, and I think that I'll stay and watch it for a while longer. Even if my bones do come to lie here beside yours in the days to come, I know that I will see the light again and that, in this life or the next, we will meet again.

Light Sinks Deep

Yes, the pirate Ocean Pearl is one of the Chosen of the Unconquered Sun, one of the Resplendent Suns, the highest and noblest of the Solar Exalted. But the higher up you are, the farther you have to fall, eh? I've watched this one carefully, through the eyes of gulls and fish and dolphins. I've even met her a few times, although never wearing the same face twice, so she doesn't suspect who or what I am.

Why do I watch her? No, not because I'm like a moth drawn to her bright flame, but because things happen around the Solar Exalted. They are giants striding across the land, and it trembles in the wake of their passing. I've seen Ocean Pearl in battle and leading her crew, and I tell you that this one may change things here in the West, so we had best be prepared and know when change is coming. If I learned nothing else in the Wyld, it's that change comes and that it's best to be ready, or else, it will sweep you away and destroy you. I've not survived this long to let my guard down now.

What changes will the Pillars of Heaven make in the world? Some of the greatest changes, I think. That's their nature. They're driven to see what is, then to see what might be and to try and make it happen. The Unconquered Sun chooses them to carry his message and to shape Creation to suit their vision of a better world. They'll discover in time that the world shapes us as much as, if not more than, we shape it. Change something, and you are changed yourself. Light a fire, and you cast a shadow. Perhaps the fire the Unconquered Sun has kindled is already casting dark shadows in the form of the Abyssal Exalted. Certainly, one of Ocean Pearl's greatest struggles will be with the Deathlords and their champions. She's already offended the honor of the Knight of Ghosts and Shadows, although I can tell that his pursuit of her is more than just a matter of duty and honor.

For now, I'll watch and see what this new light in the world will do, where her passion and her gifts will carry her. Then, when the time is right, I'll decide how to guide the change that is coming to suit our needs. Let the land worry about its own affairs. The sea is a different realm and has laws of its own, as the Resplendent Suns will soon discover.

The Sidereal Exalted

The relationship between the Sidereal Exalted and the Zenith Caste (along with the other Solar Exalted) is a complex one, driven by the different factions' interpretations of the Great Prophecy that led the Bronze faction to engineer the elimination of the other Celestial Exalted.

Now, the secret masters of the Immaculate Order and the Realm are deeply concerned by the return of the Solars. They know the Zenith Caste Solars earned the name Pillars of the Sun for their pivotal role in leading the Solar Exalted. They are the center around which the other castes gather. The Zenith are also the most zealous of the reborn Exalted in preaching to the masses and drawing people away from the guidance of the Immaculate Philosophy. Therefore, many of the Bronze faction consider the Zenith the greatest and most immediate threat posed by the Solar Exalted. Eliminate them, these Sidereals say, and the remaining Solars will be without leadership and guidance and easily dealt with. So, the Hammers of Heaven have borne much of the brunt of the Wyld Hunt's remaining attention. Fortunately for them, the Zeniths have allies and are able to withstand a great deal of punishment, and the Sidereal Exalted are finding it harder to eliminate them than they expected.

The Sidereals of the Gold faction see the potential for reuniting and empowering the Solar Exalted through the members of the Zenith Caste, provided they are properly trained and guided toward their destiny by those versed in the arts of prognostication (that is, by the Gold faction). Although the Gold Sidereals are not the enemies of the Solar Exalted, it would be naïve to call them supporters, since they have their own agenda and pursue it with the same ruthless efficiency as their Bronze faction cousins. They know the sort of havoc a member of the Zenith Caste could wreak on the nations of the world if left unchecked, and they know that grandiose statements and rebellions only serve to unite the squabbling Dynasty, which is the last thing the Gold faction wants. The Sidereals counsel patience and study and serve the members of the Zenith Caste as advisors and teachers, waiting for the time to act.

Sula

Immaculate Master,

The training of Wind, the Zenith Exalted found in Gethamane, has gone well. Whatever we may think of the work of the Bronze faction, the Immaculate Order teaches its students well. I've found Wind an apt pupil in every respect, grasping the wisdom of our ancient texts and the lore of the First Age as he if were born to it. There are still some misconceptions for us to undo, but much of the work has already been done by his

Solar nature. He apprehends the truth of who and what he is almost instinctually, guided by the Unconquered Sun as we are guided by the stars and the never-ending journey of the Maidens. If anything, the most difficult task will be reining in his enthusiasm and zeal. Having seen the truth, Wind is eager to show it to the world. Hopefully, I can make him understand that the world may not be ready for the whole truth yet.

The Cult of the Illuminated has allowed us to gather many of the newborn Solar Exalted under our guidance and teach them how to best use their gifts. But there is a matter of some concern I feel you should know. We have worked to guide the cult carefully, behind the scenes, never making our presence too well known. Many of the Solars we have recruited know there are Sidereal Exalted among the cult's ranks, that we continue to advise and aid the Solars as in ancient times. But most of the mortal followers of the cult do not know about us, only about the Solars, and even the Solars do not know the whole truth.

This may work against us. The Zenith Exalted are natural leaders, able to hold a crowd — or a cult — in the palms of their hands, and they will naturally move toward positions of leadership within the cult once they have been indoctrinated and trained. I've already seen evidence of the fanatical loyalty they can engender. What if the Zeniths wrest control of the Cult of the Illuminated from us and turn it toward their own ends, away for our sacred purpose? There may come a time when impatience and the demands of the Unconquered Sun outweigh caution and loyalty to us, their mentors.

I've done what I can to ensure that the Zeniths don't know everything they need to know in order to take control of the cult, hinting at other prophecies and ongoing divinations that we perform to keep the cult moving toward its purpose of enlightenment for all. We must continue to subtly remind the Solars — the Zenith Caste in particular — that they need our guidance and assistance, so that we can secure their loyalty for the future. I do not want to see all of our careful work spoiled by the enthusiasm of one or two Solar hotheads who decide to charge ahead and bring the wrath of the Realm down upon us. It's still too soon for us to move against the Bronze faction or the Realm yet. If you can offer me any guidance in dealing with the matter, I would be most grateful.

Respectfully,

Sula, Chosen of the Maiden of Journeys

Chejop Kejak on Dealing with the Zenith Caste

The foundation of the Zenith Caste of the Solar Exalted is built on faith: faith in themselves and the faith of others, given to their cause. In the Old Realm, the Zeniths fanned the flames of faith and inspiration within the Solar Deliberative and throughout Creation. But their faith in their own power and righteousness, and in the absolute loyalty of their subjects, grew too strong and proved to be their ultimate undoing. Faith remains the greatest weapon and the greatest weakness of the Zenith Caste even now, so it is central in dealing with them.

First, there is confidence, faith in one's self. The Zenith Caste find their faith strengthened by the favor of the Unconquered Sun, like a child given praise by a distant and stern father. They are filled with a desire to please their patron and god, to live up to his expectations of them. That inspires faith in their abilities and in their plans to help make the world a more righteous place, as they see it. Few of the Zeniths consider the far-reaching implications of their plans or their actions. Thought and deed are nearly as one with them. Of course, they are not aware of the whole truth, that their misguided efforts to save the world will ultimately doom it, nor do I imagine that anyone could convince them of it, given their self-righteous stubbornness.

The powerful passion of the Zeniths, coupled with their Charms, brings them the faith of the people to speak to and inspire. We created the Immaculate Order from an understanding of the power of faith, having seen it in action in the Old Realm. It is necessary for the people to have something to believe in, and we must ensure that it is the doctrine of the Immaculate Order and not the visions of the Blasphemous. Therein lies our means of keeping the influence we have. We must show the people that the Zeniths are, in fact, the Blasphemous, tempters luring the righteous away from the true path, which in fact they are, although not in any way we could easily explain to the common man. The leadership of the Zenith Caste will be the end of everything, unless we prevent it, so prevent it we must.

We must strike at the Zeniths through the power of faith, using it as our weapon and our battlefield. Turn their followers against them. Prepare the people for their coming, so they can resist the Zeniths' lure. Continue to spread tales of the Anathema and their dark deeds, so opinion will remain set against them. If we continue this, faith in the Zeniths will eventually crumble, and without faith, they will falter and become more vulnerable to us. To do this, we must believe in our cause as never before. The fate of all Creation rests in our hands, and it will only survive if our faith proves stronger.

The Abyssal Exalted and the Deathlords

The powers and proclivities of the Zenith Caste make them naturally opposed to the Deathlords and the Abyssal Exalted. The Zeniths wield the power of the Unconquered Sun against all forces of darkness. Their caste ability to burn corpses and keep them from rising as hungry ghosts or other restless dead is one that the Deathlords hate and fear, since it cuts directly into their power. The burning anima of one of the Resplendent Suns can send ghosts and walking dead fleeing in terror, turning aside the great armies of the Deathlords. Clearly, the Zenith Caste is a force to be reckoned with, and the Deathlords will not allow it to stand in their way.

But the lords of death are subtle and patient, and some are willing to quietly aid the Solar Exalted when they feel it furthers their own cause. Others prefer to ignore the reborn Solars or even ally themselves with the Realm to hunt them down. Certainly, no Resplendent Sun could live long within a shadowland without drawing the attention of its ruling Deathlord. Any Solar at large within their domain is a concern, but a Zenith is a definite threat, one that must be dealt with.

The greatest challenge for the Zenith Caste comes in the form of the Deathlords' champions, the Abyssal Exalted. They are the equals of the Solar Exalted in every way, making them formidable foes. Abyssal Exalted look on the Golden Bulls with caution, since they are the most likely of any of the Solars to attack Abyssal Exalted on sight as enemies of life and the Unconquered Sun. Still, some Abyssal Exalted find the passion and zeal of the Zeniths strangely attractive and are enamoured of the idea of seducing them, either to serve the cause of the Deathlords or to lure the Solars to their destruction.

Mask of Winters

Although the Solar Exalted who came to negotiate with me wisely left their Zenith brother behind, I have eyes and ears across the land, and I always know all of the people I negotiate with before we come to the table. The Zenith named Panther is known to me, as are others of his caste. He has not yet learned the wisdom of not speaking my name when he does not want me to hear, or perhaps, he did want me to hear his words or did not care if I did. That is the way of the Zeniths. They are like the thunder and the lightning: bright, loud and forceful. They strike swift and sure, stunning and dazzling those who see them act.

I also know that Panther, like many of his caste, consider the shadowlands a violation of the natural world. He would drive me and mine back across the Shroud between life and death, wielding solar fire and burning all that lay in his path. So why would I negotiate an alliance with one who may become so great an enemy? That much is simple. Panther's Circle fights to strengthen the Scavenger Lands and the River Province, so that it can stand against the forces of the Realm and become a power in its own right. A strong region is useful to me as well, and the enemy of my enemy is a useful ally.

Let the Solar Circle struggle against the forces of the Realm, without any risk to me, while I secure my hold on Thorns and spread the power of the shadowland. Whichever side wins, there is certain to be much death before it is over, and each death feeds my power and swells the ranks of my army that much more. Win or lose, I gain, and the victors are that much weaker when I must face them on the field of battle.

The Knight of Ghosts and Shadows to the Deathlord of Skullstone

Oh, Resplendent Master,

I regret that I allowed the woman Ocean Pearl to escape. I admit that I underestimated her skills, thinking her more of a figurehead able to inspire some mortal sailors and pirates. Not only is she a capable warrior, the loyalty of her crew is without question. Her first mate willingly risked his own life to help her and distracted me for the moment it took for them to escape. I promise that our next meeting will be different.

Having seen her and crossed swords with her, I am impressed by Ocean Pearl's power and skill. Master, forgive me for saying so, but it would be a terrible waste to bestow the gift of death upon her when it would rob her of her finest qualities. Although her death would end her harassment of our ships, she would be even more valuable to us if she can be made to embrace death, to welcome and love it even as I do. Then, perhaps, her power could be made to serve you, and she who was once an enemy may become a powerful ally. With your leave, I will seek out the captain of the *Scarlet Saber* again and find a way to turn her to our cause.

Her escape was useful in the sense that it not only showed us her mettle, but that of Captain Darktide as well. Although she managed to escape his grasp, Darktide fought well in your name, Master, and proved his loyalty to you. The Solar Exalted can be turned against each other, and that is a powerful weapon in our hands. Darktide may be useful in dealing with Ocean Pearl in the future, although we should still watch for any signs of sympathy for his fellow Chosen of the Unconquered Sun. Should he turn against us, Moray Darktide will feel the true embrace of death.

I remain your servant, yours to command.

The Fair Folk

The Fair Folk rarely have any sort of unified opinion about anything, including the Zenith Caste. But in general, there are two points about the Zenith that make them of interest (and concern) to the Fair Folk: their ability to inspire others and their interest in righting wrongs.

In the first case, the Fair Folk find the Zenith Caste attractive and even useful to them. The Resplendent Suns are gifted performers, able to inspire emotions and even brilliance in others, things the Fair Folk consider essential for a sublime feast of dreams and desires. Since the Fair Folk are not capable of inspiring mortals nearly so well, they are often drawn to the cults and followers of the Zenith Exalted, looking for an opportunity to feed on the dreams of their followers and even those of the Exalted themselves.

However, the members of the Zenith Caste rarely welcome the presence of the Fair Folk and don't care for them stealing the dreams and passions of their followers. Furthermore, many Solar Thunders take it upon themselves to protect mortals from the raids and "sport" of the Fair Folk, guarding cities and towns and driving the Fair Folk away from their prey. Some even go to the trouble of hunting down Fair Folk that have attacked and ravaged a place or rescuing hapless mortals who have become the Fair Folk's prisoners and slaves. This angers the faerie and makes them more likely to seek out the friends and followers of the Zenith Caste as potential victims.

Some fey see a potential use for the Zenith Caste. If many Zeniths have their way, they will eventually raise powerful armies and turn against the Dragon-Blooded and the Blessed Isle itself. A war between the Solar and Terrestrial Exalted may shatter the magical defenses that keep the Fair Folk from invading the world en masse, allowing the Shining Hosts to pour into Creation once more, and this time, nothing will drive them back. Some faerie nobles quietly support the efforts of the Solar Thunder in hopes of hastening the day when the Solar Exalted fall upon the Realm and smash its defenses.

Hayashi

The Solar Exalted have returned. Finally, prey truly worthy of the hunt! With the Dragon-Blooded clustered near their precious isle, squabbling over who will sit upon their throne, the lands on the fringes of Creation have given us considerable sport. But I grow weary of hunting rabbits and doves when I could be hunting a lioness, a veritable falcon, one of the Chosen of the Unconquered Sun. I think of what pleasure and pain, what dreams and nightmares I will be able to slowly wring from her body, mind and soul, once she is in my hands.

If only I had known what she was there beside that squat, ugly house. But then, if I had, I might have killed her too quickly. As it was, I allowed my anger to get the better of me. She struck me with iron, and the scar has not yet faded. It may always be a reminder of that day, but soon enough it will be a pleasant one as I look back on all that I did to Fire Orchid before she finally died. Yes, I allowed my anger to rule me, but it has rewarded me with this new prey, so fierce and determined. Better still, she has the endurance of the finest beasts I've ever hunted, so I know this chase will not be a short or easy one.

There may be some trouble with her allying with others of her kind. I will have to lure her out from behind the protection of her pack. But she's already given me the perfect bait. She's shown me that she cares about the mortals scurrying at her feet and praising her power and wisdom. If enough of them scream and burn, she will come running, and then, I will have her. Pour me some moonbeam and rose wine, slave, I must consider my plans.

Yirini

Oh, I remember Armattan, the Zenith who came in here some time ago, looking for a comforting touch and a passionate embrace to ease his loneliness. I especially recall the surprise on his face when he saw me. I was so tempted to try and take him for myself, but swaying one of the Zeniths from their duties and obligations can become a tiresome and even dangerous game, and I truly wasn't in the mood for it then. Still, I took some pleasure in his company and in explaining to him how I ran my house and cared for my girls and boys. I think that surprised him even more than finding me there. No doubt, he expected a huntress, stalking the dreams of mortals through the flowing silks and the sweet incense smoke, not the mistress of a house with concern for her servants and her clients.

I must give him credit. I've heard of Zeniths who would never even enter into a house of pleasure, much less one under the sway of one of the fey. He controlled his surprise well enough, and he seemed genuinely curious about my house and me, and he was never rude or impolite, like that Dragon-Blooded woman. Joyous Wren took great pleasure from his company and said that he was a lover worthy of an epic. I hope that he learned that not all of the fey are like the ravagers and the cataphractoi who raid the lands in the Threshold. Some of us still live here in peace, sustaining ourselves on dreams freely given in exchange for the pleasures we have to offer. Ah, if there had been more time, I might have shown that Zenith what some of them were....

The Spirit Courts

The reaction of spirits to the Zenith Caste is even harder to predict than that of the Fair Folk. The tendency of the Solar Thunders toward command can get them in trouble if they try to order the small gods around. Their great presence and leadership ability can gain the Zeniths the respect (or at least the cooperation) of some spirits, if they choose their words carefully. Most spirits are at least cautious when dealing with the Princes of the Earth, particularly the caste that once ruled the whole of Creation.

Bright Oasis of Traveler's Succor

He came alone through the desert, with only a lion for company, but many travelers come to me alone. He was pleasing to look upon as he quenched his thirst and cleansed himself, bending low over the water. Then, he rested under the shade of a palm. His face relaxed and became even more pleasant in sleep, as the water on him and within him called to me and I crossed the silken veil of sleep and dreams. He pursued, as men always do, his desire calling out to me, as I reached out to him.

If the beast had not woken, he would have been mine, but she roared, and he awakened in my embrace. He was more than he appeared — not just a traveler but a Prince of the Earth. They have returned! I could not stand against him. He struggled and escaped my pool, escaped my embrace and the eternal comfort I offered him. He fled into the desert, the lion at his side, and I could see there would be little comfort or rest for that one for some time. The journey is long, and the desert is harsh.

But do not worry, my dear, you are safe now. Rest within my arms, sink deep into me, and let me give you comfort and pleasure. Your journey is at an end.

Rutakin the Gatherer

Brothers! Sisters! I have seen him! One of the Princes of the Earth, here in our forest! He rests beneath the shade of Grandfather of Brilliant Jade, drinking from the pool of Water from the Roots of the World, silently meditating. Grandfather has said that he is not to be disturbed because he is one of the Chosen of the Unconquered Sun, who has sent him to us to learn his purpose. I wanted to take his bright and shiny things, but Grandfather has forbidden it. Tell everyone! This Exalted One is not to be disturbed, but to be welcomed by us here. He does not hunt wantonly and brings no fire with him, so he is well mannered, at least.

He is powerful, this one. His arms and chest bulge with muscle, and he bears the scars of many fights upon him. His limbs gleam with metal, and he carries a weapon, although he hasn't used it on anything within our forest. Play no tricks on this one, I tell you. Remember the fury of the Exalted Ones and the anger of the Unconquered Sun! Grandfather of Brilliant Jade has said he is to be left in peace and silence. I wonder if other Princes of the Earth will come here? Maybe Grandfather will let me steal from some of them, if they do.

Chapter Five
Dreams of the First Age

I stand atop a mountain and look down upon the lands of the Unconquered Sun. I look down on bountiful fields and lush forests. I look down upon glistening cities and bustling towns. I look down upon peace and prosperity. I look down upon the time before.

In the fields, farmer and animal, landowner and laborer work hand in hand to reap and sow the bounties of the earth and sun. I see plentiful harvests, abundant enough to feed to workers through the winter with enough to share with the dwellers in the cities and the towns. I see storehouses large enough to hold the bounty and farmhouses sturdy enough to shield their families against winter storms.

In the forests, hunter, predator and prey live in harmony. No beast takes more than it needs, nor kills without need. I see the deep places of the wilds where man was never meant to go, and there, I see the births of creatures that have never been seen before. I see the secret places in the wilderness where the great beasts go to die, places held in reverence by all creatures and undefiled by man.

In the cities, merchants and tradesmen live side by side. Craftsmen and artisans do not want for materials. The rich and the aristocratic walk among the common men willingly. All manner of goods are plentiful in the city, from the simplest of foods to the rarest of art. The cities are sparkling jewels of wonder, filled with miraculous devices and magnificent structures, drawing visitors from the far corners of the land. Newcomers, visitors and natives alike are free from the ravages of crime, and yet, the hand of its rulers does not rest heavy on the land.

In the towns, the traditions are remembered and followed with reverence. Respect is paid to the elders by the youths, and the elders rear the youths to be worthy of respect. Though their temples are modest, the folk of towns remember to worship their gods according to the proper times and seasons. Sons and daughters study at the feet of their parents, learning the professions that had been dictated by the ancestors. Mothers and fathers respect their children's wishes when they wish to follow their own path.

I stand atop the highest mountain and look down upon the unblemished lands of the Unconquered Sun. I look down upon the time before.

* * * * *

I look to the south, and I see a crystal spire rising out of the wilderness. Taller than any other building in the land, the tower acts as both beacon to and watch tower for those who dwell in its shadow. The structure glows with an inner light both day and night, as if the sun had allowed a bit of itself to be stored within. I see movement within and fly closer to see who could dwell in such a place, to see what activities could grace such a tower.

As I near the crystal spire, I see that the tower does not stand alone. Five lesser crystalline structures encircle the glowing peak; five crystal domes complete this landbound constellation. I circle the structures, peering into each of the domes.

The first dome glows with the green of life. Peering inside, I see all manner of farms. The second rings with the clash of metal on metal. Inside, warriors train against one another daily. I smell sulfur and smoke as I fly past the third dome. There, craftsmen endlessly create new wonders from jade and gold and ivory. The air about the fourth dome is sweet with the taste of sugars and chocolates, for this dome is home to great chefs and bakers who create all manner of culinary treats. The final dome is smooth and peaceful. Inside, quiet gardens provide a place for repose and memorial of the ancestors.

I fly ever closer to crystal spire. A great circle of stones provides the base of the tower. Inside the circle, the greatest philosophers of the age gather to discuss and record the secrets of life. Fresh-faced students gather at the feet of wizened masters. Scribes record discussions, and stonecutters inscribe the great truths at the direction of the greatest of savants. Oh, how I long to tarry hear and listen to their words.

Yet, I continue to travel along, through the circle of philosophers and up into the tower. As I rise further and further, the wonders I behold increase. I see rooms lit by bits of borrowed sunlight. I hear songs emanating from invisible orchestras. I smell flowers where none can be found. Further and further up, I fly. Ah, what an orderly tower. Exalted live above unExalted. Nobles dwell above commoners and royalty dwell above nobility.

Finally, I reach the zenith. Here, the mightiest and noblest in the land meet to discuss the fate of those below. Here, the glow of borrowed sunlight is the brightest. From here, one can see the far corners of the land. I pause at the top and peer back along the path I followed. Ah, the wonders we have lost. Ah, the wonders that we can hope to regain.

* * * * *

From the wilderness, a voice beckons me. Following the sound, I travel across plains and over hills. I plumb the depths of valleys and climb the heights of mountains. On and on, I travel, and yet, the voice beckons. At long last, I reach a dark and primeval forest — one far more primal than any I have ever encountered before. I enter the wood, and onward, the voice beckons. I climb over fallen trees and wind my through thick and knotted vines. Finally, I come to a clearing; I come to the source of the voice.

Standing just inside the clearing, I gaze upon a wondrous sight. I see an ancient tree, teeming with all manner of life. The mass of animals upon its trunk moves constantly, making the tree seem a noble beast itself. There are creatures tending the tree and the soil around it, providing food for the tree and the animals that call it home. I see creatures watching over the workers, protecting them and the tree from harm and resolving disruptions before they affect the society. I watch as, high in the tops of the tree, wondrous and beautiful creatures — feathered and furred and scaled — give orders and accept tribute, all for the betterment of the tree as a whole.

As I watch, a great tigress springs forth from the tree, roaring and snarling. At her call, a dozen other animals leave their duties at the trunk and in the branches and fall in behind the great cat. Moving, as if of one mind, the creatures move to strike at a foe that I had yet to detect. A great darkness had been forming, subtly, at the edge of my sight, but before it could even set its tendrils, the she-cat led her warriors against it. Though the darkness was larger than the beasts, the animals attacked fearlessly, and the darkness fell, defeated.

From the shadows of the tree, a great spider leaps, marked in bright reds and dark blues. The animals of the tree pay deference to the arachnid, and the spider springs immediately to work. The eight-legged one works tireless, spinning a web from the poorly lit branches of the tree. I gaze in wonder as the delicate threads capture and hold the sunlight, glowing in response to the sun's warm caress. The web glows softly but provides a comforting light to the creatures that live and work near it.

A great wolf leaps from the shadows near the tree. Skulking in the shadows, avoiding even the spider's light, the wolf patrols places that my eyes had left unseen. All the animals of the tree watch the creature with a respectful dread. The wolf winds his way through the branches, watching those beasts that seem lax in their work. His mere passage is enough to revitalize some. I watch in awe as the wolf encounters a beast that is stealing from its fellows and hoarding food for itself. With a single smooth action, the greedy beast has vanished, swallowed whole by the vengeful wolf.

A piercing scream draws my eyes upward. There, I see a great falcon, circling the tree. I watch as the silver bird flies in and around the tree's outstretched branches, pausing here and there where other animals are having disputes. Wherever the great bird's shadow passes, arguments are solved and peace is restored.

Finally, a great golden bull leaps from the tree. All work on the tree stops as each creature turns to see what the bull might do. I watch in amazement as the bull drops his horns in respect to the tree. Then, in turn, each of the tree's dwellers bends its knee in respect to the bull. First, the workers; then, the watchers; and then, the noble creatures that dwell high in the tree's branches show their respect to the great bull. Finally, the great beasts come before the golden creature, the mighty tiger, the clever spider, the mysterious falcon and even the skulking wolf.

I realize the beckoning voices have gone silent, and treasuring the things I had seen, I return along the path I had come.

* * * * *

I look to the North and see a city on the ice, where no city has any right to be. Curious, I investigate, racing along, north and north and north until I reach the ice-locked town. Unseen and unheard, I walk among its inhabitants, gazing at its wonders. Though the air must be bitter cold to maintain the streets of hoarfrost on which my fellow wanderers and I tread, they seem not to feel the chill. I wonder at this, as they wear garments of cloth that, though strange to my eye, seems as light as summer cotton.

I gaze at open-air shops, where artisans work bare armed and, yet, in comfort. A cheery warm glow fills the air of the storefronts. Customers and friends pause before each one to admire the workmanship and to exchange news. Though the air in these places is clearly much warmer, the shoppers make the transition from the cold streets to the cheery shops with no discomfort. They merely pull the cloth that covers their faces aside, to facilitate conversation.

I am curious as to what other miracles this city has to offer and wander onward, invisibly sharing the road with the natives of this place. I walk further on and come to a building marked with a sign of a thread and needle. Hopeful that I might find the secret of the cold-resistant cloth, I travel inside. In the building, I see rows and rows of skeins of cloth. I see more colors and patterns than I have seen in any one place before. I work my way through the collection, wondering where such bounty could come from. I ascend a spiral staircase. On the second floor, I see a collection of lead and gold machines whirring along with clockwork precision. From the ceiling, threads descend into the equipment. Ornately patterned clothes flow from the apparatuses. But from whence do the threads come? I climb yet another spiral staircase. At the top level of the building, a crystal dome caps the floor, separating the treasures here from the cold night air. I see delicate trees covered in gold and opal flowers. Women wander through the garden, tending the plants. Others draw multicolored threads from the flowers and feed them into golden boxes at the base of each tree. So, the wonderful cloth comes from thread grown on trees. Even as one mystery was solved, another presents itself.

I peered out of the glass dome, wondering what fed these people in this frozen wasteland. As I did, I saw another series of crystal-topped structures, glowing green. Surely, this garden provided enough cloth, even for a city this size. Then what was tended in those buildings? With a gentle leap, I am launched harmlessly through the dome and across the night sky. My leap ended as I passed through the green domes without leaving mark of my passage. I looked about and saw plants hanging in midair everywhere. Fine tendrils spill gently downward. Fruits of all types grow from heavier vines. Thick moss grows on the thickest of vines. I watch workers gather both the fruit and the moss and give it to waiting deliverymen. I float above, watching the deliverymen transport the moss and fruits to every home in the city. Another mystery solved, but how many more remain to be discovered in this frozen city?

* * * * *

I find myself riding the waves far out to sea. I dance with the creatures of the depths as I drift to where the horizon meets the sky. There, I see a city of ships, forming three great circles around a golden pyramid with steps leading to the sky. I ride the waves and draw ever closer to the curious sea-borne city.

The great ships of the sea make up the outermost circle. These craft are far larger than any I have ever seen before. They are too massive to make use of even the largest port I was familiar with — ships large enough to carry small villages of their own. Traders dicker on these sea craft, buying and selling vast amounts of supplies from all corners of the globe.

The second circle is made up of a collection of smaller ships. Materials from the great ships are loaded onto these ships. I describe these ships as smaller, but upon closer inspection, I realize they are as large as the big ships that I am familiar with in the waking world. This circle of ships is somewhat fluid, as these craft leave their places in the circle and make their way out to the open sea, squeezing through gaps between the great ships.

Even smaller ships make up the innermost circle. These ships are lashed together in three arcs. Merchants and pilgrims alike move from ship-to-ship, and goods and services are available on the ships. I am reminded of the merchants that gather outside the temples in the cities of my youth. Yet, where my memories are of greed and dishonesty, these merchants seem somehow noble.

Smaller craft yet navigate between and around all of the ships, all of the circles, and back and forth from the great pyramid. Travelers ride these small boats like land-dwelling men ride horses. Merchants from the middle ring travel to the inner ring. Pilgrims from the inner ring travel to the pyramid. I follow the pilgrims inward, and once I reach the pyramid, I pursue the travelers as they make their way up the steps. Up and up I travel, following the path of the devout. Some are satisfied to pause only partway up, to be tended by the lesser priests at the lower levels. Others continue further up. At each level, more and more pause to be tended by higher- and higher-ranked priests. Further and further up I go, until only the most dedicated of pilgrims remain on the journey. There stands the high priest, glowing with the inner light of the sun. As my sojourn ends, I watch as golden healing extends from the high priest to the devout.

* * * * *

I awake in unfamiliar surroundings. The sky is aglow with multicolored lights, the air is filled with appetizing smells, and gleeful noises ring in my ears. I arise from my bed, which disappears, and my sleeping clothes are replaced with a festival costume. I wander through the streets, rubbing elbows with frenzied partiers.

I wonder at the joy around me. What lord would allow his people to celebrate so freely? What wealth must he possess that he can afford the extravagance displayed here and afford the loss of work such a festival surely implies? Surely, the master of this place must be attempting to impress a rival with this display of generosity. I continue to wander, trying to make sense of the events around me.

I stroll down crowded streets and see food merchants of all kinds. I see great sides of meat cooking over glowing bars of metal. Creations of sugared ice, treats normally reserved for nobility, are displayed proudly, kept from melting inside glass boxes. I see multicolored fishes, rolled together with grains and grasses into works of culinary art, yet this city does not lay by the sea. Breads of all shapes and sizes, a wide variety of sausages and vegetables both mundane and exotic are on sale around another corner.

I continue at a casual pace, exploring the festival with eyes full of wonder. I see and hear performers of all sorts, both wandering musicians thrilling passers-by and small orchestras attracting crowds from fixed stages. I tarry a bit to enjoy strains of

music familiar to my ears. These are tunes that were ancient in my youth, yet the crowds thrill to them as if they are new and still exciting.

As the music continues to play, I find myself rising above the revelers. I float above the crowds as they spill out of the city and into the surrounding plains. As the festival reaches a fever pitch, the partiers don masks. I see bulls and tigers and spiders and falcons and wolves among the dancers who spin outward in ever-widening spirals. The musicians gather together and join the dancers on the plains. Colored fire explodes above and around me, as the music becomes louder and louder. From my airborne vantage point, I watch as the dancers trace ornate paths over and over on the ground. I am enchanted by the dance and feel myself pulled downward into the patterns. I fly faster and faster, lost in an explosion of color and sound.

I awake in my bed, alone in quiet and squalor.

* * * * *

I find myself wandering in a great city carved from stone. Wonders of art surround me. Statues decorate the thoroughfares and the rooftops. The architecture is ornate and yet, somehow, perfectly aligned. As I gasp at the wonders around me, my feet carry me, unbidden, into one of the buildings.

I find myself in an arched hallway. The walls are lined with books, more than I've ever seen before, but it is the ceiling that draws my attention. If I were not aware that I was standing inside, I would state without doubt that I was peering at the early morning sky. As I walk further down the hall, the ceiling changes with me. I watch, as the sun seems to rise, chasing away the colors of the night. Further and further on I walk, as the morning sky gives way to the brightly lit sky of midday. The artistry above me is without question magnificent, for, at times, I believe I can see the clouds in the painting moving. On and on, I walk, amazed as the midday gives way to late afternoon and as the purples and reds of evening creep into view. It is then that the hall opens into a room. The ceiling of the chamber depicts the night sky, as accurately as the hall depicted the skies of the day. Peering about the rest of the room, I find it dominated by a statue that can only represent the Unconquered Sun.

As I peer in wonder at the statue, lights fill the room from unseen sources. Some flicker across the great statue, making it seem as if the mighty statue moves, while other motes of light dance across the ceiling. I watch in wonder and amazement as I recognize the dancing lights. First, a single light circles above. It is a soft light, all silvery and full of mystery. I can only assume that I watch Luna's eternal ballet. Soon, five other lights join it, each a different color. These new lights weave complicated patterns across the would-be sky. Each dancing color follows a distinct pattern, and yet, the patterns intersect in a harmonious way. I know that I am watching the Maidens, or at least colors intended to represent the Maidens.

"Fascinating, fascinating." I hear a dry old voice echo through the room. I become aware of the scratch, scratch, scratch of a quill on parchment. "I've not seen the ladies dance like this before. Fascinating." I tear my eyes away from the dancing lights to seek out the speaker. As my vision adjusts to the darkness, I see a figure working at a small desk in a cubbyhole on the opposite side of the Unconquered Sun statue from me. "But I can't have these dates right. This conjunction won't happen for years and years." I see the glint of metal. The man works with a brush of fine ermine, but there is no inkwell to be seen. I try to ask what he means, but I find my voice silent and the room already fading from my sight.

* * * * *

Again, I find myself wandering the great city carved from stone, and again, I find myself wondering at its statues. Once more, I find my feet carrying me forward unbidden, my destination not of my choosing.

With a quick step, I pass through a door into a cluttered hall. The first thing I become clearly aware of is the smell of the place. I smell rotten eggs and the air after a lightning strike. Intense smells, but somehow, in this place, they are not overwhelming. There are old smells here, and the atmosphere of the building treats them like old friends. They belong here, perhaps more than I do.

I move through the hall past open doors to cluttered rooms. It seems that no surface is left uncovered here. Those areas not covered with bits of metal are littered with books, left casually about — how someone could treat such valuable texts so carelessly amazes me.

From further down the corridor, I can hear the sound of banging and hissing. Though I fear some great beast intent on destroying this place and all within it, my feet carry me ever closer. The noises continue, growing ever louder as I near their source. The air in this place is powdery and tastes somewhat like dust but, somehow, more sharp. The air tingles, and alternating blasts of warm and cold air blow against me as I walk down the hall.

I pass more rooms, and it slowly dawns on me that the bits of metal littering the rooms are in fact sculptures, some of things recognizable, others of things strange to me. I see mechanical cats and birds with wings made of bits of copper and geometric figures made from iron and from gold. Yet, my feet draw me on before I can stop to investigate them further.

Drawing ever closer to the din at the end of the hall, my heart fills with dread. Is it my imagination, or do I see some of these metallic creations moving of their own volition? Onward and onward, I tread. The door separating me from the noise opens on its own. I try to close my eyes against the terrors I know lay beyond, but I cannot.

Inside, I see a great metal man. Steam hisses from his joints. His chest is open, and inside, I see a massive hammer swinging back and forth. At each end of the hammer's arc, it stops with a loud clang. As I enter the room, the bronze giant slowly stands. Is it reacting to my presence, moving to strike me down as the invader I am? I look fearfully into the construct's face hoping to divine its intentions. The metallic monster has the head of a bull but eyes as glassy as a corpse. Though I look it straight in the eyes, it does not appear to see me.

Behind the bronze giant, I become aware of a soot-covered woman, working feverishly. "What is the purpose of this creation?" I try to speak, but no words come from my mouth. Already, my time here seems to have passed.

* * * * *

Once again, I find myself in the city with statues of marble and buildings of the purest stone. I become aware that each of the buildings has windows made of glass. What a wondrous place, what extravagance! Some of the windows even have bits of colored glass arranged in patterns. Though I cannot interpret all of the patterns, I realize that the colored glass depicts the purpose of each building. Amazed by my discovery, and used to my uncontrolled travels in this city, I wander on without care.

I pause in front of a particular door. Glancing to my right and to my left, I see twin windows. Human forms are depicted in the colored glass, with an icon of the golden sun superimposed on their chests. I am allowed little time to wonder what might lie inside, as, with a step, I am through the door.

The hall is well lit. The brightness of the place causes me to blink, to allow my eyes to adjust. All of the surfaces seem crisp and clean. Everything seems new. There is a smell in the air that I cannot place — a smell not unlike alcohol, but, somehow, more pure. I do not know its source, but breathing it leaves a pleasant aftertaste in my mouth, and I feel somehow cleansed. The air is cool, but comfortable, and its flow is gentle but continuous. So soft is the breeze that I am barely aware of the movement against my skin, and it is only the movement of the leaves of a nearby plant that gives the breeze away.

It strikes me. I see an indoor plant. The image of it fixes in my mind. It is green and healthy. It is healthier than any plant in the richest of soils, and it is not alone. A dozen such plants line the hallway, hanging from the ceiling by fine ropes.

I become acutely aware of my heart beating, of its thrumb, thrumb, thrumb in my ears. I continue down the hall as my unbidden feet carry me forward. I pause and turn to peer through a glass wall. No, I am peering through a pair of doors made of glass. Beyond them, I see beds. At least, I think they are beds. The frames are made of what looks like the finest silver, and the sheets look like the finest silk. Who would sleep in such beds?

Before I can examine the beds further, my feet have already started along their mysterious path anew. I walk further down the hall, toward a set of mirrored doors that slide open as I approach. I stride through them without hesitation to where two men wait, garbed in simple white robes. One lies on another silver bed, this time without the silk sheets. The other stands over him, looking at him. The standing man reaches over to a well-polished counter and retrieves a finely crafted knife. I watch in mute horror as the standing man draws the blade across the prone man's chest. The image fades before I can see any more.

* * * * *

My family goes to sleep without food. That which I intended to feed them was taken from us. The madame has raised the taxes again, and her representative took the last of what we had stored in payment. We were told that we would lose the hovel we call a home next. I go to sleep on straw, my stomach complaining.

I awake in comfort, in a lord's bed, thoughts of hunger a distant memory, a faint and faraway dream. I am wearing bedclothes, and I can see clean work clothes hanging on a peg on the wall. I dress in silence and wonder. Surely, this is some sick prank, played by Madame Aesh for her amusement or the amusement of guests, but I fear not to play along, in dread of some worse punishment. Cautiously, I leave the sleeping room and enter the rooms beyond.

The kitchen is clean and comfortable. The sun's warm glow beams in through a paper window. Bread and cheese sit on a cutting board on the table, along with a sharp knife. I see a sack sitting nearby and cut myself generous helpings of the food. Some I eat now, fearful that the game will end too soon, the rest I put in the bag. Perhaps I can take it home to my loved ones when this is all over.

Game or no, I must tend to my duties to the land. Princes come and madames go, but we belong to the land, and it is the land that holds my loyalties after my kin. I pause at the door to unlatch it. I fumble a bit, as I am not familiar with the lock. Soon, however, the door is open, and I go outside to greet the morning sun.

I am amazed by what I see. Though it is the land I know, the land I've worked and my ancestors have worked and their ancestors have worked, it has been transformed overnight. The cracked and barren soil that I had turned every day for years in hopes of coaxing life from it was suddenly lush and rich. Plants grew thick in the black earth. I could see blood-red fruit and golden pods, all nicely arranged and separated into neat rows.

I walk along the rows, tugging at solitary weeds. The soil releases them willingly, and the task is more of a joy than a chore. My eye is attracted by a series of pipes, running near to the ground and along the rows. I follow them along, smaller pipes connecting to larger pipes until I reach the edge of my ancestral land. There, an even larger pipe waits, marked with some lord's seal. Curious, I follow the pipes back to the plants and watch as they begin to drip with water, providing moisture in the dry season.

I awake cold and wet and hungry. My family and I went to bed hungry, the last of our food stolen by the madame's tax collector.

* * * * *

I stand at the podium, my arms spread wide. I am clad in cloth of orichalcum, and a weight hangs heavy about my neck — the Ring of the Deliberative, the torc that marks me as the spokesman and servant of the Unconquered Sun. Three Hearthstones glitter within it; a Gem of Incomparable Wellness, a Gem of Sapphire and Emerald and the Hearthstone from the Imperial Manse, whose possession gives the bearer complete control over the defenses of the Realm.

Before me lies the assembled Solar Host and the Lunar Society and the nameless gathering of the Sidereals, their eyes glittering like stars from the vast balcony. Delegates of the Dragon-Blooded daimyos are here as well and representatives of the bureaucratic organs.

I step forward to the podium, glancing left and right at my four fellow Deliberators. I open my mouth to speak, and as I speak, I know my words are lies.

It is a petty matter, the distribution of subsidies to Celestial Exalted who do not rule principalities. The reason for the lie is equally petty — to secure greater subsidies for Solars and especially for members of the Deliberative. "We have spoken with Unconquered Sun, and he agrees." And that is the lie that we are not permitted.

In my heart, I can feel the affronted face of my god, my patron, turning away from me, yet I speak anyway. Dreaming, I cannot understand why it is I do what I do, yet I do it anyway. Perhaps I am mad, or perhaps I truly think that I am so great that I can use a god's name merely to validate my own decisions.

My fellow Deliberators ritually lower their heads, the long nod that signals they are in agreement with the speaker on matters of faith. They, too, are lying, but like me, they do not realize what it portends. I awaken with a start in the stifling space behind the old scroll racks and sigh. The dream will come again, as it always does.

Chapter Six
Magic of the Zenith

The Exalted are beings of vast magical power. Though, in theory, any Solar is able to master nearly any Ability, most develop powers that emphasize their personal focus, a focus typically closely related to their caste. This was true in the First Age as well, and of the sorcerous artifacts that were created in that lost time, many are clearly designed to aid the Exalted in performing their roles. This chapter details some of the powers and the artifacts that were used primarily by members of the Zenith Caste. Characters may learn of or discover these Charms, artifacts and Hearthstones, or they may invent them or create them independently; this chapter should serve as a resource to both Storytellers and players.

Charms

Endurance

Empty Stomach Fasting Meditation

Cost: 1 mote
Duration: One day
Type: Simple
Minimum Endurance: 1
Minimum Essence: 1
Prerequisite Charms: None

The constitutions of Exalted are far more resilient than those of mere mortals, yet even the Chosen must eat. Through the use of this Charm, an Exalted may eliminate her need to eat for a single day. Activation of this Charm takes the normal investment of Essence and meditation for one-quarter hour. Use of this Charm does not alleviate the need to drink water. The Charm may be used for up to 40 days in a row without penalty. Afterward, the Chosen must eat and drink normally for three days in a row. This Charm will not work again until the Chosen has so eaten.

Ascetic Monk's Purification Discipline

Cost: 10 motes
Duration: Three days
Type: Simple
Minimum Endurance: 3
Minimum Essence: 3
Prerequisite Charms: Empty Stomach Fasting Meditation

In the harsh conditions of the wilderness, even fresh water can be hard to come by. The Exalted who has mastered this Charm can go without food and water for three days. Activation of this Charm takes the normal investment of Essence and meditation for a full hour. The Exalt must eat and drink normally for at least one day before this Charm can be used again.

Controlled Breathing Exercise

Cost: 5 motes
Duration: One scene
Type: Simple
Minimum Endurance: 2
Minimum Essence: 2
Prerequisite Charms: None

The Exalted uses Essence to reduce his need for breathing. Once the Charm is activated, the Chosen need not breath until the scene is over, as long as he does not speak and only attempts simple actions. Each turn the Exalted attempts a complicated action, including combat, he must make a reflexive Stamina + Endurance roll to avoid breathing. Obviously, this Charm is of great use in poisoned environments.

Sleep of Death Technique

Cost: 15 motes
Duration: Special
Type: Simple
Minimum Endurance: 4
Minimum Essence: 4
Prerequisite Charms: Controlled Breathing Exercise

Through the use of this Charm, an Exalted can give the illusion of death. Her heartbeat slows to imperceptibility, and she does not breath. To every mortal inspection, the Chosen is dead. The Exalted can remain in this state for as long as she chooses, but the Charm does not remove the need to eat or drink, putting a practical limit on its use without the invocation of additional Charms.

Unsleeping Watchman Technique

Cost: 5 motes
Duration: One night
Type: Simple
Minimum Endurance: 2
Minimum Essence: 2
Prerequisite Charms: None

Even the most careful of Exalted must sleep sometime, and it is when they sleep that they are most vulnerable. The use of this Charm replaces the need for a night's sleep with spent Essence, allowing the Exalt to act without penalty both day and night. There is no limitation on the number of concurrent days on which the Charm may be used. However, each night that Unsleeping Watchman Technique is invoked is a night without dreaming. After a number of consecutive days equal to the Chosen's Stamina + Endurance, the Exalted will begin to experience waking dreams, seeing and hearing weird, seemingly disconnected objects and sounds. Mechanically, the distraction of these hallucinations will cause the character to suffer a one die penalty on all checks. This penalty increases by one day for each additional period of (Stamina + Endurance) consecutive days.

Tireless Runner's Stride

Cost: 10 motes
Duration: Special
Type: Simple
Minimum Endurance: 3
Minimum Essence: 3
Prerequisite Charms: Unsleeping Watchman Technique

An Exalted with Tireless Runner's Stride can run for an extended period to complete her tasks. The Chosen must have a specific target in mind when invoking the Charm and must invest the Essence as normal. Afterward, the Exalted can run without ceasing until her goal is reached. She needs no sleep, nor does she need to perform bodily functions. If a sufficient supply of food and water is carried, the Exalted may eat and drink without stopping or slowing her running speed. Her pace is tripled by the investiture of Essence and by the lack of need to stop. If the Exalted stops running, the Charm ends. This running prevents the Exalt from regaining Essence naturally, just like any other strenuous exercise. The Exalted must clearly know the location she seeks to properly invoke this Charm.

Extended Life Prana

Cost: None
Duration: Permanent
Type: Special
Minimum Endurance: 7
Minimum Essence: 7
Prerequisite Charms: Empty Stomach Fasting Meditation, Sleep of Death Technique, Tireless Runner's Stride

The Exalted who masters this Charm has his natural life extended many times, staving off the reaper with his righteousness. While the typical Solar Exalted lives for 2,000 to 3,000 years, this Charm extends his life to 5,000 to 7,000 years. The possessor of this Charm shows no sign of aging or degradation of health until his very last days walking Creation. This Charm offers no protection from damage or disease, it merely extends the lifespan of the Chosen. In addition to the prerequisites listed above, the Exalted must have a rating of at least three in all of his Virtues.

Resistance

Environmental Hazard-Resisting Meditation

Cost: None
Duration: Permanent
Type: Special
Minimum Resistance: 5
Minimum Essence: 2
Prerequisite Charms: None

Some Exalted, in their years of wandering the wilderness, develop an immunity to nature's rigors. To simulate this, a character can take this Charm to grant permanent resistance to one of the following conditions. Each time she purchases this Charm, she can choose one of the following:

- Resistance to Extreme Heat
- Resistance to Extreme Cold
- Resistance to Acid
- Resistance to Windblown Particles

A character with one of these resistances suffers no damage from natural occurrences of the condition and is comfortable acting in it wearing normal gear. For instance, a Chosen with Resistance to Extreme Heat may walk across the most brutal of deserts without penalty, but still suffers damage if caught in a forest fire or magical flame. This Charm is similar to Ox-Body Technique, in that an Exalt can take it repeatedly, until she has purchased all four versions. A character cannot purchase this Charm more times than she has dots in the Resistance Ability.

Alcohol-Resisting Prana

Cost:	1 mote
Duration:	One scene
Type:	Simple
Minimum Resistance:	1
Minimum Essence:	1
Prerequisite Charms:	None

By invoking this Charm, the Exalted becomes immune to the negative effects of alcohol for the rest of the scene. He suffers no penalties during or after the scene in which Alcohol-Resisting Prana is used, and in fact, the effect is quite pleasant, as the character experiences the euphoric feelings of drunkenness without any of the impairment normally associated with heavy drinking. If the character is already drunk, then all negative effects of the alcohol are negated until the Charm ends. In addition, invoking this Charm prevents any chance of hangover from alcohol drunk during the scene, whether or not the Charm was in effect when the alcohol was consumed.

Drunken Warrior Technique

Cost:	2 motes
Duration:	Instant
Type:	Reflexive
Minimum Resistance:	2
Minimum Performance:	2
Minimum Essence:	1
Prerequisite Charms:	Alcohol-Resisting Prana

The Drunken Warrior Technique allows the invoking Exalted to harness the unpredictability of drunkenness in combat. When this Charm is invoked, the character may add dice to an attempt to attack or an attempt to dodge or to parry an attack. The Charm may

be invoked multiple times per turn, but the total number of dice added in a given turn cannot exceed the number of drinks the character has had during the scene or the sum of the character's Resistance and Performance Abilities, whichever is lower.

For the purposes of this Charm, a "drink" is a glass of wine, a tankard of beer, a dram of hard liquor or the equivalent. This Charm does not provide any immunity to the negative effects of drinking, but may be used even if the alcohol's effects have been negated though the use of the Alcohol-Resisting Prana.

Inebriated Fool Defense

Cost: 2 motes
Duration: Instant
Type: Reflexive
Minimum Resistance: 4
Minimum Performance: 3
Minimum Essence: 1
Prerequisite Charms: Drunken Warrior Technique, Spirit Strengthens the Skin

The Inebriated Fool Defense allows the Exalted to utilize the effects alcohol has on the human body, loosening its muscles and joints, to withstand damage. When this Charm is invoked, the character may add a number of points to his bashing soak equal the number of drinks he has consumed during the scene. This number can be no greater than the sum of the Exalted's Resistance and Performance Abilities. The Charm may be invoked multiple times per turn, and the bonus is the same each time it is invoked. The effects of this Charm are compatible with other Resistance Charms that increase the character's bashing soak.

For the purposes of this Charm, a "drink" is a glass of wine, a tankard of beer, a dram of hard liquor or the equivalent. This Charm does not provide any immunity to the negative effects of drinking, but may be used even if the alcohol's effects have been negated though the use of the Alcohol-Resisting Prana.

Interrogation-Resisting Attitude

Cost: 5 motes
Duration: One scene
Type: Simple
Minimum Resistance: 2
Minimum Essence: 1
Prerequisite Charms: None

The character's will and body are strengthened by Essence, allowing her to easily endure all forms of torture and interrogation. The player may add a number of automatic successes equal to the character's permanent Essence to any Resistance rolls to avoid breaking under interrogation. The character need not call upon this power before the interrogation and may even invoke it after giving some information during the interrogation.

Use of this Charm does not negate the effects of any toxins used in the interrogation, nor does it prevent damage. It merely allows the character complete control over what she chooses to say.

Pain-Reducing Meditation

Cost: 1 mote per -1
Duration: One scene
Type: Reflexive
Minimum Resistance: 3
Minimum Essence: 2
Prerequisite Charms: Interrogation-Resisting Attitude, Durability of Oak Meditation

The cumulative effects of pain can bring down even the hardiest of Exalted. This Charm allows a Chosen to ignore pain through the application of Essence. To activate the Charm, the Exalted chooses to what degree he wishes to ignore wound penalties for the remainder of the scene. For each –1 wound penalty the character ignores, the Charm costs 1 mote to activate. This Charm may be used multiple times during a single scene, with cumulative effects. A character can also negate more points of wound penalties than he is currently suffering, to anesthetize himself against later injury.

Armor of Virtue Technique

Cost: 3 motes
Duration: One scene
Type: Simple
Minimum Resistance: 2
Minimum Essence: 2
Prerequisite Charms: Durability of Oak Meditation

Through the expenditure of Essence, this Charm allows the Exalted to reinforce his ability to withstand attack with one of his Virtues. The character must choose the Virtue at the beginning of the scene and act in accordance with that Virtue for the duration of the scene. If at any point he acts contrary to the chosen Virtue, the Armor of Virtue fades immediately. Specifically, attempting any action that would require failing a Virtue check causes the Charm's effects to expire. For example, abandoning or attempting to abandon a loved one to perish miserably while under the protection of Compassion causes the Armor of Virtue to fail.

When invoked, the Armor of Virtue Technique increases the character's bashing soak by the value of the character's chosen Virtue for the rest of the scene. This Charm may be used again on subsequent turns, but a character cannot gain a greater bonus to his bashing soak via Armor of Virtue Technique than his Stamina + Resistance. The effects of this Charm are compatible with the effects of other Resistance Charms that increase the character's soak.

While under the effect of the Armor of Virtue Technique, the Exalted's Caste Mark glows brightly, as if the character had spent 4 to 7 motes of Peripheral Essence. Invoking this Charm automatically adds one point to the character's Limit.

Fivefold Armor of Virtue Technique

Cost: 5 motes
Duration: One scene
Type: Simple
Minimum Resistance: 3
Minimum Essence: 3
Prerequisite Charms: Armor of Virtue Technique

Through the expenditure of Essence, the Fivefold Armor of Virtue Technique allows the Exalted to reinforce his ability to withstand attack with one of his Virtues. The character must choose the Virtue at the beginning of the scene and act in accordance with it for the duration of the scene. If at any point he acts contrary to the chosen virtue, the Fivefold Armor of Virtue fades immediately, as per the Armor of Virtue Technique.

When invoked, the Fivefold Armor of Virtue Technique increases the character's lethal soak roll by the value of the character's chosen Virtue for the rest of the scene. This Charm may be used again on subsequent turns, but a character cannot gain a greater bonus to his lethal soak via Fivefold Armor of Virtue than his Stamina + Resistance.

While under the effect of the Fivefold Armor of Virtue Technique, the Exalted's anima glows brightly enough to read by, as if the character had spent 8 to 10 motes of Peripheral Essence. Characters wearing armor cannot use this Charm. Invoking this Charm automatically adds one point to the character's Limit.

Survival

Storm Warden Concentration

Cost: 6 motes
Duration: One day
Type: Simple
Minimum Survival: 3
Minimum Essence: 1
Prerequisite Charms: Hardship-Surviving Mendicant Spirit

This Charm protects the invoker from the adverse affects of natural weather. The Exalted may move through heavy winds without being impeded by them, travel through a sand- or snowstorm without being blinded or spend a stormy night with no shelter without fear of becoming waterlogged. The Chosen's anima deflects these conditions, providing a nearly skintight zone of protection for the Exalted and any possessions worn against her body. This Charm does not protect against damage from temperature extremes.

Salamander's Touch Technique

Cost: 1 mote
Duration: Instant
Type: Simple
Minimum Survival: 3
Minimum Essence: 2
Prerequisite Charms: Hardship-Surviving Mendicant Spirit

Through the use of this Charm, the Exalted can light small, controlled fires. These are normal fires in every way. They can cause no damage by themselves, but if allowed to blaze out of control, they can be as dangerous as any other fire. The fires this Charm can light are limited to normally flammable materials. The Charm is useless against water-soaked wood or other noncombustible substances.

Unquenchable Conflagration Technique

Cost: 10 motes
Duration: Instant
Type: Simple
Minimum Survival: 3
Minimum Essence: 2
Prerequisite Charms: Salamander's Touch Technique

When all the available wood is soaked or, worse, when there is no wood to be found, even the most skilled survivalist can find herself forced to live without heat and flame. This Charm allows the Exalted to cause a fire of up to bonfire size to spring into existence with but a gesture. The fire will burn for a complete scene, even in high winds or driving rain, but it will not spread unless normally flammable materials are introduced. This power cannot be used as a direct attack.

Sun's Flaming Tongue Attack

Cost: 15 motes, 1 Willpower
Duration: Instant
Type: Simple
Minimum Survival: 5
Minimum Essence: 3
Prerequisite Charms: Unquenchable Conflagration Technique

Through the use of this Charm, the Exalted rains down solar fire upon a single opponent. After investing the required Essence, make a Willpower roll. The fire does a number of points of lethal damage equal to the Exalted's Survival score, plus one point of damage per success on the character's Willpower roll. This power can strike at a range of line of sight. Against demons, ghosts or other creatures of the night, the damage is aggravated. This attack cannot normally be blocked or dodged, but targets may have Charms that allow them to do either in their defense.

Game-Snaring Huntsman's Method

Cost: 1 mote per die
Duration: One day
Type: Supplemental
Minimum Survival: 4
Minimum Essence: 1
Prerequisite Charms: Hardship-Surviving Mendicant Spirit

When invoking this Charm, the Exalted names a single breed of animal, which may include "human." He then crafts a snare appropriate for trapping the species of interest. For each mote invested in the Charm, the Survival roll to create the snare is increased by one die. In addition, for each mote invested, the targeted breed suffers a one-die penalty to detect or escape the trap. The trap will not be triggered by any species other than the one named. This trap cannot be used to snare a specific specimen, but instead, affects the first member of the species that encounters it.

Game-Snaring Huntsman's Method cannot be used to create a trap that will innately do damage, such as spike-pits or deadfalls. It can only be used to enhance snares, pit traps and the like. If incidental damage is done to a target in escaping the trap, then the trap may still be eligible for the Game-Snaring Huntsman's Method.

Devil-Pit Technique

Cost: 2 motes per die
Duration: One week
Type: Supplemental
Minimum Survival: 4
Minimum Essence: 2
Prerequisite Charms: Game-Snaring Huntsman's Method

The Devil-Pit Technique functions in many ways like the Game-Snaring Huntsman's Method. The Exalted names a breed of animal to be targeted by the trap. The roll for creating the trap is increased by one die for every 2 motes invested in the Charm, and the targeted breed suffers a like number of dice in penalty for rolls to detect or escape the trap. The trap will not be triggered by any species other than the named one, nor can it be set to trap a specific individual.

Unlike Game-Snaring Huntsman's Method, Devil-Pit Technique can be used to enhance traps that are designed to cause damage or death to their targets, rather than restrain them. A trap enhanced by the Devil-Pit Technique does one die of soakable lethal damage per 2 motes invested in the Charm. This damage is in addition to any damage a normal trap of the design might do.

Performance

Gender-Concealing Meditation

Cost: 5 motes
Duration: One day
Type: Simple
Minimum Performance: 3
Minimum Essence: 1
Prerequisite Charms: Phantom-Conjuring Performance

Sometimes, there are places that a woman can go that a man cannot, and vice-versa. This Charm helps an Exalted overcome such problems through disguise. By applying Essence to the task, the Chosen can enhance his illusion of femininity (or her illusion of masculinity). The application of Essence reshapes the Exalt's body into the proper curves and leaves those who might see his or her sex organs with the impression that they were those of the opposite gender. The Charm will not fool close physical examination and does not allow intercourse, but anyone doing a less thorough inspection will be deceived.

Graceful Reed Dancing

Cost: 2 motes per success
Duration: Instant
Type: Supplemental
Minimum Performance: 2
Minimum Essence: 1
Prerequisite Charms: None

The character channels Essence through his body, enhancing his sense of rhythm and making his dance a riveting display. To use this Charm, the character must be performing a dance. The player first makes a regular Charisma + Performance roll for the character. Then, the player may "buy" additional successes, up to (the character's permanent Essence rating + the number of successes rolled on his Charisma + Performance roll). Each success bought in this fashion costs 2 motes of Essence. Graceful Reed Dancing is not compatible with Masterful Performance Exercise, as it is basically the same Charm for a different mode of Performance.

Husband-Seducing Demon's Dance

Cost: 5 motes
Duration: One scene
Type: Simple
Minimum Performance: 4
Minimum Essence: 2
Prerequisite Charms: Gender-Concealing Meditation, Graceful Reed Dancing

This Charm raises the art of seduction through dance to a supernatural level. So long as an Exalt using this Charm continues to dance, all who watch the performance see him or her as the most desirable being possible, regardless of their sexual preference. They are unwilling to harm the Chosen and are likely to behave irrationally in an attempt to impress the Solar. This Charm is ineffective on beings with an Essence higher than the Exalted invoking the power. The Charm does not work on characters who are in combat or who otherwise have reason to believe the Exalt means them harm. Overtly hostile acts on the part of the dancing character dispel the Charm's effect.

Divine Performance Style

Cost:	10 motes
Duration:	Special
Type:	Simple
Minimum Performance:	5
Minimum Essence:	3
Prerequisite Charms:	Husband-Seducing Demon's Dance

By combining song and dance with the art of seduction, the Exalted invoking this Charm weaves a spell of influence over a chosen target. Like Husband-Seducing Demon's Dance, this Charm starts with a masterful performance by the Exalted. This performance includes both song and dance and is directed at a specific individual. Regardless of the specific genders of the Exalted and the target, the target will be entranced by the extreme desirability of the performer.

Other observers of the Divine Performance will be affected much as if observing the Husband-Seducing Demon's Dance, but the Charm will have no overt effect on them. Against the chosen target, however, there is an extended effect. The Exalt's player rolls Charisma + Performance and compares the resulting number of successes against the target's permanent Willpower. Other Charms may be used to enhance this Performance roll, including the Masterful Performance Exercise.

If the Chosen achieves more successes than the target's permanent Willpower, the target will be particularly vulnerable to the influence of the performer for a number of days. The duration of this influence is equal to the difference between the Exalt's permanent Essence and the target's. While under the influence of the Divine Performance, a victim is at a –1 Essence with regard to the use of mind-controlling or -affecting Charms by the Exalt. For example, if the Exalted achieves 10 successes against a target with a Willpower of 7, the target will be at a -1 Essence penalty for 3 days.

Beings with Essence 1 who have their Essence reduced become the infatuated thralls of the Exalt for the duration of the effect. They will not kill themselves (though they may easily be manipulated into doing so), but they will perform almost any other act, even the most foolish or foolhardy.

The Essence penalty does not stack with other uses of Divine Performance Style, but the Exalt can use Divine Performance again before a previous application has expired to extend its duration. In this case, the new result replaces the older one, even if it is lower. With proper planning, an Exalted performer can keep one or more targets entranced indefinitely.

King of Masks Technique

Cost: Special
Duration: Special
Type: Simple
Minimum Performance: 3
Minimum Essence: 1
Prerequisite Charms: None

Through the use of this Charm, the Exalted weaves a complicated false identity around herself. The identity is complete with a detailed history and natural personality traits. Mere conversation cannot detect any flaws in the identity. In fact, the infallibility of the identity is perfect until the Exalted chooses to drop the façade or she is faced with an investigative intellect that is likewise Charm-enhanced. King of Masks Technique provides no resistance to interrogation techniques.

When invoking the Charm, the Exalted crafts a back-story for herself and her player makes a Intelligence + Performance roll, adding one automatic success for each mote of Essence she chooses to invest. The total number of successes is the number of successes an investigator must achieve to see through the false identity, but this can never exceed twice the character's Intelligence + Performance pool. Only Charm-enhanced Investigation rolls will reduce this pool of successes, but all such investigations are cumulative. The Fair Folk and beings with Essence higher than the character are immune to the effects of this Charm.

At the time of an identity's creation, the Exalted may spend one experience point to make the identity permanent. The character may resume a permanent identity at any time by spending half as many motes of Essence as she originally spent creating the identity. Persistent investigators can wear away at and eventually destroy permanent identities. If an identity is pierced, then the experience point is lost. Permanent identities can be investigated even when the character is not using them. Motes of Essence spent creating a permanent identity are not committed after the identity is first "put aside," but whenever the character resumes the identity, the Essence she pays to resume it is committed while she uses the identity.

This Charm cannot be used to mimic specific individuals. It can only create fictional identities. An Exalted may have as many permanent identities as she has points of permanent Essence.

Impenetrable Identity

Cost: 10+ motes, 1 experience point
Duration: Special
Type: Simple
Minimum Performance: 5
Minimum Presence: 3
Minimum Essence: 2
Prerequisite Charms: King of Masks Technique

Impenetrable Identity is initially identical to King of Masks Technique, but with some significant enhancements. First of all, while using Impenetrable Identity, the Exalted becomes the role he has chosen. While the Charm is in effect, he consciously and even subconsciously believes he is the role he has adopted. Interrogation techniques that do not have a magical basis are useless for discovering the Chosen's true identity because the character has no idea that he is not his cover identity.

When invoking the Charm, the Exalted crafts a back-story for himself and makes a Intelligence + Performance roll, adding two automatic successes for each mote of Essence, beyond the base cost of 10, she chooses to invest. As with King of Masks Technique, the number of successes can never exceed twice the character's Intelligence + Performance pool. Normal investigation and interrogation is useless against Impenetrable Identity, and when Charm-enhanced interrogation or investigation is used to attack an Impenetrable Identity, only half the investigator's successes, rounded down, count for reducing the success pool.

At the time the Charm is invoked, the Chosen may set any number of conditions that will automatically restore her original identity. This can include a time period, arrival at a specific location, spoken key words or any other triggering event that the character chooses to specify prior to assuming the Impenetrable Identity. There can be as many triggering conditions as the character wishes, and if they are at all complex, they should be written down to prevent disputes. The identity also ends automatically if anyone can pierce it and prove it to be false. When the identity ends, it is gone forever, and the experience point is lost.

Presence

Impassioned Orator Technique

Cost: 5 motes
Duration: One turn
Type: Supplemental
Minimum Presence: 3
Minimum Essence: 2
Prerequisite Charms: Listener-Swaying Argument

An Exalted acting in accordance with virtue is an impressive figure indeed — an Exalted using this Charm is even more so. By using this Charm, the Chosen puts the weight of her passions behind her arguments. She may add one of her Virtue ratings in automatic successes to a single Presence roll. The Virtue may be chosen when the Charm is invoked, but the Exalted must be acting in accordance with the virtue in question. If the Exalted is not, or does not, act according to the Virtue, the Essence is spent, but no bonus is gained. Invoking this Charm automatically adds one point to the character's Limit.

Countenance of Vast Wrath

Cost:	10 motes
Duration:	One scene
Type:	Simple
Minimum Presence:	4
Minimum Essence:	2
Prerequisite Charms:	Impassioned Orator Technique

When driven by his passions, an Exalted can be an almost irresistible force. Through the use of this Charm, one of the Chosen may spend Essence to let the strength of her virtue strike fear in the hearts of those who would oppose her. For the remainder of the Scene, any character with a Willpower lower than the Exalted's current Limit suffers a penalty to his dice pools equal to the Exalt's Essence when attempting to attack her. Invoking this Charm automatically adds one point to the character's Limit, which counts toward the character's Limit for the purposes of determining this Charm's effect.

Hearthstones and Artifacts

Hearthstones

Eye of the First Goat

(Earth, Manse •)

Trigger: Non-combat situations

This pale-orange stone has a slitted red "eye" in its center. The Eye grants the possessor a bonus to Athletics rolls equal to one-half his Temperance, rounded-up. In addition, if the Eye of the First Goat is set in a blunt weapon, it grants the owner a one-die bonus to any melee attacks made with that weapon.

Jewel of the Flying Heart

(Air, Manse •)

Trigger: Combat

This blood-red stone has a number of sharp facets. The Jewel grants the possessor a bonus to Dodge rolls equal to one-half her Conviction, rounded-up. In addition, if the Jewel of the Flying Heart is set in an edged weapon, it grants the owner a one-die bonus to any melee attacks made with that weapon.

Stone of the Emerald Rooster

(Wood, Manse •)

Trigger: Constant

This stone is primarily green but has rainbow sheen in the noonday sun. The Hearthstone grants a bonus on all Survival and Endurance rolls equal to one-half the possessor's Valor, rounded-up.

Gem of the Noble Brook

(Water, Manse •)

Trigger: None, constant

This pale-pink stone is delicate and smooth. While carried, the possessor cannot have a poor Social Trait. If the carrier has an Appearance, Manipulation or Charisma of 1, the Trait is raised to 2. As soon as the stone is removed from the owner's presence, the Trait reverts to its original level.

Jewel of the Clever Merchant

(Air, Manse ••)

Trigger: Business negotiations

This silvery-white stone carries many complex facets. The bearer of this stone gains a three-die bonus to all rolls associated with business negotiations, including price dickering, contract negotiation and bidding for rights. This bonus can be applied to both Mental and Social rolls.

Jewel of the Rabbit's Sword

(Lunar, Manse •••)

Trigger: Expenditure of Willpower

This sharply faceted stone is yellow-green in color, and its shape and number of facets seem to change rapidly. The possessor may expend one temporary point of Willpower to reroll any 1's in any Ability check. This power may only be invoked once per Ability check.

Sphere of the Revolutionary Dog

(Fire, Manse •••)

Trigger: Constant

This orb is a brilliant orange, and it appears to be filled with slowly billowing tongues of flame. This sphere increases the rate at which temporary Willpower is regained. Any time the owner recovers Willpower for any reason, the amount of Willpower regained is increased by one. This bonus will never raise the character's temporary Willpower above his permanent Willpower.

Sphere of Courtesan's Constellation (Solar, Manse •••)

Trigger: None, constant

This perfectly spherical orange stone is filled with golden flecks. If the possessor of this stone has an Appearance of 2 or lower, the Trait is raised to 3. As soon as the stone is removed from the owner's presence, the Trait reverts to its original level. In addition, the possessor of the sphere gets a two-die bonus to all Performance and Presence rolls.

Gemstone of the White Jade Tree (Earth, Manse •••)

Trigger: Constant

This blue-violet stone seems to glow with an inner light. Any damage suffered (after soak) by the possessor is halved, rounding all fractions up. At the same time, the possessor's Dexterity pool and movement speed are halved, rounding down.

Stone of Healer's Flower (Wood, Manse ••••)

Trigger: Concentration, touch

This is a simple blue stone. At will, the possessor of this stone may touch any other individual and heal their wounds completely. Anyone who has ever used this stone to heal another is immune to its healing affects. The possessor of this stone immediately suffers half the damage she healed (rounded up), which cannot be negated, redirected or otherwise reduced. This damage must be healed normally and may lead to the bearer's death. At the same time, the bearer of the stone may roll a number of dice equal to the number of health levels suffered. Each die success reduces the bearer's Limit by one point.

Jewel of the Monkey's Finger (Lunar, Manse ••••)

Trigger: Constant

This round stone is a deep violet. This jewel adds two dice to all Dexterity and Charisma rolls made by the possessor's player. In addition, while leaping and capering like a monkey, the owner of this stone may use his Dexterity and Charisma scores interchangeably. While this can prove a massive boon to an Exalted who finds himself particularly blessed or limited in one of these areas, jumping and frolicking are not suitable under all circumstances. The Storyteller should feel free to increase the difficulty of appropriate checks by one or more dice in situations when monkey-like behavior would be a detriment.

First Age Artifacts

All artifacts in this section are constructed from orichalcum unless otherwise noted.

Heavenly Thunder Leaves (Artifact • each)

These ornate wind-fire wheels have a speed rating of +3, an accuracy rating of +2, a damage rating of +0 and a defense rating of +5. In addition, if they are used as part of a dancing performance, they add a one-die bonus to any Performance rolls made by the owner's player.

Heavenly thunder leaves do not appear to be standard wind-fire wheels. Instead, they look like carefully painted dancing fans. They depict a forest of flowering trees during a lightning storm. In the forest, young lovers and spirits frolic. There is a dance that tells the tale depicted on the fans, and when done properly, the dance will attract the attention of nearby spirits, moved by the beauty of the story and the talent of the dancer. Make a Dexterity + Performance dancing roll for the possessor of the fans to invoke this effect. If the check results in at least three successes, any little gods within 100 yards become aware of the dance and the dancer.

The little gods will be at least neutrally inclined toward the dancer and will move to within speaking distance of the dancer. Each success above three in the initial Performance roll grants a one-die bonus to the next Social roll made for the performer to influence the attendant spirits. The fans confer no special abilities to see or communicate with the spirits.

No bonus of any sort is gained if only one of the fans is possessed or used. It costs 2 motes of Essence to attune to each of the wheels.

Death Shield Ring (Artifact •••)

This ring has a setting for a single Hearthstone. In addition, while worn, the ring grants the wearer the ability to survive any single attack that would result in death. If the wearer would normally be slain from the damage of an attack, the ring explodes in a brilliant flash of light, and the damage is not inflicted. The ring is completely consumed by this effect. If there is a Hearthstone set in the ring, it is cracked by the ring's destruction.

Reborn Glacial Rain (Artifact •••)

This knife appears to be made of pure glacial ice, and it has a speed rating of +9, an accuracy rating of +2, a damage rating of +7L and a defense rating of +0. The bearer of this blade also gains some significant advantages in polar environments. All Survival checks made in arctic terrain receive a three-die bonus, as do any Resistance or Endurance checks related to survival in cold climes.

Reborn Glacial Rain has a setting for a single Hearthstone. According to the tales, if it can be found, this blade will be the second incarnation of a legendary weapon. During the First Age, Glacial Rain was destroyed when Vaznia of the Night Caste used its blade to slit the throat of one of the Yozis. It costs 5 motes to attune to Reborn Glacial Rain.

Flying Silver Dream (Artifact ••••)

This ornate, straight-bladed moonsilver daiklave has a speed rating of +3, an accuracy rating of +4, a damage rating of +10L and a defense rating of +3. Upon command, Flying Silver Dream will leap from its bearer's hand and attempt to engage an opponent, named by its attuned wielder, in single combat. When fighting on its own, the sword is considered to have Attributes and Abilities equal to the character who launched it and a movement speed figured as normal from its Dexterity. It acts on its wielder's initiative.

The sword will fight until its target is slain, its bearer mentally commands it to return (a reflexive action) or its wielder is incapacitated. While the sword is fighting on its own, its wielder may engage in battle using another weapon, use Charms or participate in any other activity he chooses. If the sword kills its target and the wielder is otherwise occupied, it will orbit him until he commands it to attack a new target or until he has a hand free to take possession of it.

Anyone who wishes to attack Flying Silver Dream while it fights on its own may do so as if it were a character — it dodges with 12 dice, and all attackers automatically subtract 2 successes from their attack rolls to reflect the difficulty of hitting the whirling weapon. Flying Silver Dream automatically dodges all attacks without penalty to its normal actions and without a reduction in its dice pool for subsequent attacks. Flying Silver Dream has a 10L/8B soak, and any attacker must do at least three damage successes to it to have any effect. If the sword does take three levels in one attack, it drops to the ground, undamaged but unable to fight again until its wielder picks it up and commands to it to do so (picking it up is a dice action).

In addition, this item has a setting for a single Hearthstone. It costs 5 motes to attune to Flying Silver Dream. Flying Silver Dream is designed so that Solars or Lunars can receive the moonsilver Material bonus when attuned to it.

The Ring of the Deliberative (Artifact •••••)

This elaborate torc has settings for three Hearthstones and was once worn by the Hierophant of the Solar Deliberative when he executed official business. The wearer of the neck-ring gains a five-die bonus to all Zenith Caste Ability checks and a two-die bonus to all Social Attribute checks that do not involve the Zenith Caste Abilities. The bearer appears to be greater than he is. He seems to be bigger and stronger, his features seem more distinct and handsome. His gear seems to be more valuable and better-tended. In short, he appears to be an Exalted among Exalted.

Appendix I
Signature Characters

The Hammers of Heaven are the mouths of the Unconquered Sun and the spiritual leaders of the Solar Exalted. Even before their Exaltations, each had immense potential as a leader, a survivor and a missionary. Each is given a vision of her place in the world by the Unconquered Sun himself, and each is hero enough to take up that mission. Yet, each is still an individual, and the Unconquered Sun does not dictate solutions to his servants. The Zenith Caste are left to seek a righteous world as they know best, and that breeds conflict as well as strength.

This book presents the points of view and stories of five of the Pillars of the Sun, and this appendix provides the statistics for those narrators, described as if they were starting characters of the Zenith Caste. They can provide inspiration for players' characters, or they can provide ready-made Storyteller characters, to be used either unaltered as novice heroes or (with added Charms and Combos and increased Abilities) as a base for depicting more experienced Exalted.

Panther

Quote: *The world can be made pure and whole once again, and it starts here.*

Prelude: Growing up in Nexus, you never knew your father, and your mother died when you were a boy. You stole to survive until you were captured and sold into gladiatorial slavery. You fought so many battles that you lost count. You fought men and beasts, armed and unarmed. Ultimately, you won your freedom from slavery through blood and death. However, given your freedom, you turned your back on the world and walked back into the arena, the only world you ever knew.

As a free gladiator, you fought and won great victories. You had your fill of money, wine and women, but inside, you felt only emptiness. All of your victories turned to ash before your eyes. When your Exaltation came upon you, it was as if you had wakened from a long slumber, as if your life until then was merely a half-remembered dream. Your senses were suddenly more alive than ever before. You gathered only what you needed and ventured into world, turning your back on the arena without a second thought. You walked into the forest without fear, guided and guarded by the Unconquered Sun. There, in the silence, for the first and last time, you questioned why you were chosen. You realized that you had been chosen because you had always been seeking a purpose. You know what has to be done. Now, all that remains is for you to do it.

Roleplaying Hints: Having experienced the best and worst that life can offer, you know that the purity of the Solars, and of the Zenith in particular, is the purity of hard work, the purity of hot sweat that purges poison from the body. You, who had no father, now have the Sun as your father. With newfound purpose, you venture forth into the world to make it a righteous place. Totally committed, you have never looked back. You know that if you are to be a beacon of righteousness to the world, then it must be through your actions, not your words. You believe that the future of the world will be forged in the Scavenger Lands. You believe that the Dragon-Blooded need not be your enemies. You believe the greatest threats come from the Wyld — the destructive barbarians, the dangerous Fair Folk, the vengeful Lunar Exalted. You may have been trained as a warrior, but you serve your Circle as a diplomat.

Image: Panther was always larger and stronger than his contemporaries, and his days as a gladiator only served to strengthen his build. His skin is dusky brown, and he moves with the grace of a hunting cat.

Equipment: Slayer khatars, common clothes, bag full of jade

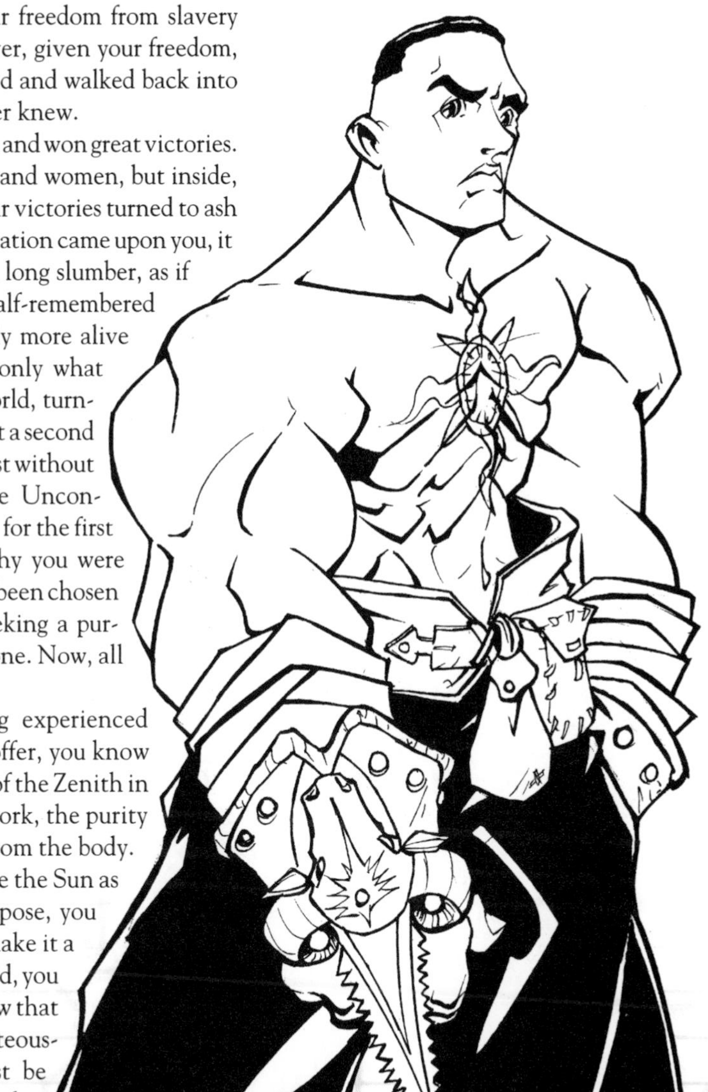

EXALTED

Name: PANTHER
Player:
Caste: ZENITH
Concept: PIT FIGHTER
Nature: ARCHITECT
Anima:

Attributes

Strength	●●●○○	Charisma	●●●○○	Perception	●●○○○
Dexterity	●●●●○	Manipulation	●●●○○	Intelligence	●●○○○
Stamina	●●●●○	Appearance	●●●○○	Wits	●●●○○

Abilities

Dawn		Zenith		Twilight	
☐ Archery	○○○○○	■ Endurance	●●●○○	☐ Craft	○○○○○
■ Brawl	●●●●○	■ Performance	●●○○○	☐ Investigation	○○○○○
☐ Martial Arts	○○○○○	■ Presence	●○○○○	☐ Lore	○○○○○
☐ Melee	●○○○○	■ Resistance	●●●○○	■ Medicine	●○○○○
☐ Thrown	○○○○○	■ Survival	●○○○○	☐ Occult	○○○○○

Night		Eclipse		Specialties	
■ Athletics	●●○○○	☐ Bureaucracy	○○○○○	☐	○○○○○
■ Awareness	●●○○○	☐ Linguistics	●●○○○	☐	○○○○○
■ Dodge	●●○○○	☐ Ride	○○○○○	☐	○○○○○
☐ Larceny	●○○○○	☐ Sail	○○○○○	☐	○○○○○
☐ Stealth	○○○○○	☐ Socialize	●○○○○	☐	○○○○○

Advantages

Backgrounds

ARTIFACT	●●○○○
RESOURCES	●●●○○
INFLUENCE	●●○○○
	○○○○○
	○○○○○
	○○○○○
	○○○○○
	○○○○○
	○○○○○
	○○○○○

Name	Cost
FEROCIOUS JAB	1
FIST OF IRON TECHNIQUE	1
OX-STUNNING BLOW	1/DIE
THUNDERCLAP RUSH ATTACK	3
HAMMER ON IRON TECHNIQUE	4, 1W
OX-BODY TECHNIQUE	SPEC

Name	Cost
SLEDGEHAMMER FIST PUNCH	3
DURABILITY OF OAK MEDITATION	1/2 DICE
IRON SKIN CONCENTRATION	3, 1W
BODY MENDING MEDITATION	10

Weapons

SLAYER KHATAR
SPD 4 ACC 8 DMG 5L PRY 7

Willpower

●●●●●○○○○○
☐☐☐☐☐☐☐☐☐☐

Virtues

Compassion ●●●○○ ☐☐☐☐☐
Temperance ●●○○○ ☐☐☐☐☐
Conviction ●●●○○ ☐☐☐☐☐
Valor ●●●○○ ☐☐☐☐☐

Anima

Health

Soak
B 4 L 2 A 0

-0	☐☐☐☐☐
-1	☐☐■■■
-2	☐☐■■■
	☐☐■■■
-4	☐
Incapacitated	☐

Essence

●●●○○○

Personal 15 |
Peripheral 37 |
Committed

Limit Break

☐☐☐☐☐☐☐☐☐☐

Virtue Flaw

RED RAGE OF COMPASSION

Experience

Ocean Pearl

Quote: *My name is Ocean Pearl, captain of the* Scarlet Saber. *Ah, so you know her name if not mine, eh? Well, you'll be hearing mine soon enough.*

Prelude: You knew that you were born to the sea from the time you were only a girl. As soon as you were able, you ran away from home with little more than the clothes on your back. You went to a small seaport town and sought commission on board a ship as a cabin girl. You sailed with an old sea captain on the Western Ocean and the Inland Sea, until you encountered the pirate Blackheart, the Man With No Shadow. Your ship was captured, and you were to be given as prize to Blackheart's master. Blackheart may have had no heart and no shadow, but he was a man in every other way, and you were able to strike a bargain with the pirate. You became the lover of a man with no heart and became a pirate as well.

You may have only been Blackheart's mistress, but you gained a measure of power on board his ship and something resembling his trust as well. You won the admiration and respect of the crew, in part due to your ability to sometimes mollify Blackheart's anger. Despite the proven invincibility of the captain, you decided to attempt the impossible. You knew which members of the crew to talk to. Once you gathered a cadre of trustworthy allies, you coaxed the secret of his power out of Blackheart. Now was the time. As you prepared to free the world of Blackheart, the Unconquered Sun freed you from your own bondage. Bathed in the golden light of the Sun, your sword was like a scythe in your hand. You cut your way through Blackheart's loyal men and, finally, dispatched the Captain himself. Since then, you have raided the ships of the Realm and the Guild.

Roleplaying Hints: You're not just a pirate. You are a rebel against the Realm and all of its allies. You work against the rulers of the world and inspire the people for the future. You don't care for the term "mortal." The worth of a person comes from their actions, not their lifespans. You prefer the company of your crew to most immortals and have learned the hard way that not all of the Chosen of the Sun further the cause of righteousness in the world.

Image: Ocean Pearl, despite being weathered by the sea and tempered by battle, is a woman who can still turn a man's head.

Equipment: The *Scarlet Saber*, slashing sword, various silks and treasures taken as booty, leather buff jacket

EXALTED

Name: OCEAN PEARL
Player:
Caste: ZENITH
Concept: ROBIN HOOD
Nature: REBEL
Anima:

Attributes

Strength	●●●○○	Charisma	●●●●○	Perception	●●○○○
Dexterity	●●●○○	Manipulation	●●●○○	Intelligence	●●●○○
Stamina	●●●○○	Appearance	●●●●○	Wits	●●○○○

Abilities

DAWN		ZENITH		TWILIGHT	
☐ Archery	○○○○○	■ Endurance	●○○○○	☐ Craft	○○○○○
☐ Brawl	●○○○○	■ Performance	●●○○○	☐ Investigation	○○○○○
☐ Martial Arts	○○○○○	■ Presence	●●●●○	☐ Lore	○○○○○
■ Melee	●●●○○	■ Resistance	●●○○○	☐ Medicine	○○○○○
☐ Thrown	●○○○○	■ Survival	●○○○○	■ Occult	●○○○○

NIGHT		ECLIPSE		SPECIALTIES	
■ Athletics	●●○○○	☐ Bureaucracy	○○○○○	☐	○○○○○
■ Awareness	●●○○○	☐ Linguistics	●●○○○	☐	○○○○○
☐ Dodge	●○○○○	☐ Ride	○○○○○	☐	○○○○○
☐ Larceny	●●○○○	■ Sail	●●●○○	☐	○○○○○
☐ Stealth	●○○○○	☐ Socialize	○○○○○	☐	○○○○○

Advantages

Backgrounds

FOLLOWERS	●●●●●
RESOURCES	●●●○○
ALLIES	●○○○○
	○○○○○
	○○○○○
	○○○○○
	○○○○○
	○○○○○
	○○○○○
	○○○○○

Name	Cost
SALTY DOG METHOD	3
PERFECT RECKONING TECHNIQUE	4
WIND-DEFYING COURSE TECHNIQUE	6
SHIPWRECK-SURVIVING STAMINA	5
RESPECT-COMMANDING ATTITUDE	5

Name	Cost
HARMONIOUS PRESENCE MEDITATION	6
OX-BODY TECHINQUE	SPEC
EXCELLENT STRIKE	1/DIE
HUNGRY TIGER TECHNIQUE	1M
GOLDEN ESSENCE BLOCK	1/2 DICE

Weapons

SLASHING SWORD
SPD 8 ACC 7 DMG 5L PRY 7

Willpower

●●●●●○○○○○
☐☐☐☐☐☐☐☐☐☐

Virtues

Compassion ●●○○○ ☐☐☐☐☐
Temperance ●●○○○ ☐☐☐☐☐
Conviction ●●●○○ ☐☐☐☐☐
Valor ●●○○○ ☐☐☐☐☐

Anima

Health

SOAK
B 7 L 4 A 3
-1 MOBILITY PENALTY

-0	☐■■■■
-1	☐☐☐☐■
-2	☐☐■■■
	■■■■■
-4	☐
Incapacitated	☐

Essence

●●●○○○

Personal 15 |
Peripheral 35 |
Committed

Limit Break

☐☐☐☐☐☐☐☐☐☐

Virtue Flaw

DELIBERATE CRUELTY

Experience

Armattan

Quote: *I have business in this city, and I've come a long way to get here. Once my business is concluded, I'll leave, but not before.*

Prelude: Originally from Gem, you served for a time as a caravan guard. Sometimes, the caravans you guarded would encounter bandits, great cats or even sand swimmers. You survived them all. It was during your last caravan trip that things changed. It was summer, and the caravan traveled by night, when the desert cooled, thankful for the warmth of the sand against the chill in the air. During this trip, the raiders came upon you without warning and by night, while you traveled. You were injured in the attack, and you slashed your attacker with your khatar, tearing his robes and cutting his sword-arm. The pommel of his sword met your skull with a crack, and blackness claimed you.

You awoke to the screeching of carrion birds gathered to feast and felt the burning heat of the sun on your back. You were alone, your companions all dead, and the caravan looted of everything of value. Raising your fist to Heaven, you swore vengeance against your attackers. At that moment, you were Exalted. The signs of the bandits' passing were suddenly as clear to you as the blazing sun overhead. As you walked, ever with more surety, the pain from your wound troubled you less, and the burning heat of the sun on your back became a gentle, soothing warmth. You did not walk far before you were joined in your travels by a desert lion. You felt a sense of recognition and kinship with the proud beast. An understanding passed between you, and the lioness joined your journey as your companion.

Roleplaying Hints: You have seen visions of the First Age. You have seen visions of great battles and heroes. You have seen visions of betrayal and grave injustice. Now, you carry the message of the Sun to the world of men. You are filled with energy and purpose. Sometimes, people do get the chance to save the whole world, like the Scarlet Empress did from the Fair Folk, but most of the time, it's just a matter of helping one person or one village at a time. If the Realm were a place of justice and righteousness, you would support its rule. You have fought at the side of the Dragon-Blooded for the sake of justice, but you would fight against them for the same reason.

Image: Armattan's skin looks like worn leather as a result of years spent guarding caravans under the hot sun. A nasty scar marks his side as a reminder of his Exaltation.

Equipment: Khatar, a desert lion named Sirah, a pocket full of recovered gems

EXALTED

Name: ARMATTAN
Player:
Caste: ZENITH
Concept: CARAVAN GUARD
Nature: SURVIVOR
Anima:

Attributes

Strength	●●○○○	Charisma	●●●○○	Perception	●●●●○
Dexterity	●●●○○	Manipulation	●●○○○	Intelligence	●●●○○
Stamina	●●●●○	Appearance	●●○○○	Wits	●●●●○

Abilities

Dawn		Zenith		Twilight	
☐ Archery	●○○○○	■ Endurance	●●●○○	☐ Craft	○○○○○
☐ Brawl	●○○○○	■ Performance	○○○○○	☐ Investigation	○○○○○
☐ Martial Arts	○○○○○	■ Presence	●○○○○	☐ Lore	○○○○○
■ Melee	●●○○○	■ Resistance	●●○○○	☐ Medicine	●○○○○
☐ Thrown	○○○○○	■ Survival	●●●○○	☐ Occult	○○○○○

Night		Eclipse		Specialties	
☐ Athletics	●○○○○	☐ Bureaucracy	○○○○○	☐	○○○○○
■ Awareness	●●●○○	☐ Linguistics	●○○○○	☐	○○○○○
■ Dodge	●●●○○	☐ Ride	●○○○○	☐	○○○○○
■ Larceny	●○○○○	☐ Sail	○○○○○	☐	○○○○○
■ Stealth	●●○○○	☐ Socialize	●○○○○	☐	○○○○○

Advantages

Backgrounds

FAMILIAR	●●●●○
RESOURCES	●●○○○
CONTACTS	●●○○○
	○○○○○
	○○○○○
	○○○○○
	○○○○○
	○○○○○
	○○○○○
	○○○○○

Name	Cost
OX-BODY TECHNIQUE	Spec
BODY MENDING MEDITATION	10
HARDSHIP-SURVIVING MENDICANT SPIRIT	5
TRACKLESS REGION NAVIGATION CHARM	7
UNSHAKEABLE BLOOD-HOUNDTECHNIQUE	8, 1W

Name	Cost
SENSORY ACUITY PRANA	5
DURABILITY OF OAK MEDITATION	1/2 DICE
IRON SKIN CONCENTRATION	3, 1W 1/DIE
EXCELLENT STRIKE	1
HUNGRY TIGER TECH.	1/2 DICE
REED IN THE WIND	

Weapons

KHATAR
SPD 4 ACC 5 DMG 4L PRY 4

Willpower

● ● ● ● ● ○ ○ ○ ○ ○
☐ ☐ ☐ ☐ ☐ ☐ ☐ ☐ ☐ ☐

Virtues

Compassion	Temperance
●●○○○	●●○○○
☐☐☐☐☐	☐☐☐☐☐

Conviction	Valor
●●○○○	●●●○○
☐☐☐☐☐	☐☐☐☐☐

Anima

Health

Soak
B 4 L 2 A 0

-0	☐■■■■
-1	☐☐☐■■
-2	☐☐■■■
	☐☐■■■
-4	☐
Incapacitated	☐

Essence

● ● ● ○ ○ ○

Personal 14 |
Peripheral 35 |
Committed

Limit Break

☐ ☐ ☐ ☐ ☐ ☐ ☐ ☐ ☐ ☐

Virtue Flaw

FOOLHARDY CONTEMPT

Experience

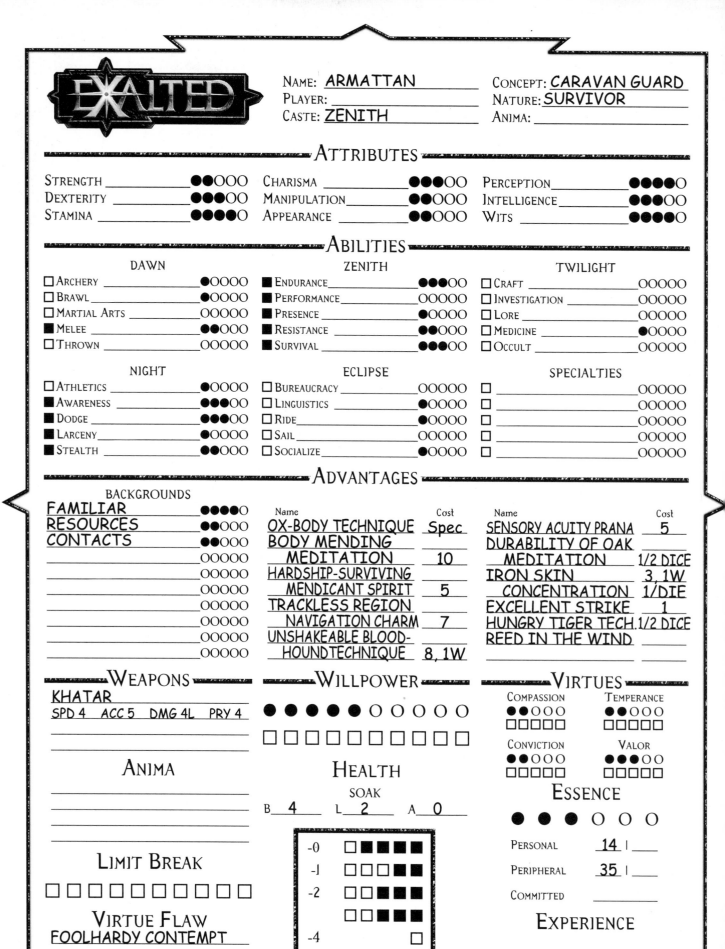

Karal Fire Orchid

Quote: *Back! Back! I am the Chosen of the Unconquered Sun! Away from here, or feel my blade!*

Prelude: Your mother named you Fire Orchid because she said you were as beautiful as a blossom but had a fire burning within you. Your mother was respected by you and acknowledged as one of Lookshy's greatest generals. Out of love for your mother, you were a good example to your brothers and a responsible older sister. When it was learned that you were not among the Dragon-Blooded, you held your head high in public but cried yourself to sleep at night. To prove yourself, you struggled through mud and mire, waded through blood, charged through fire, all while upholding the standard of the Seventh Legion faithfully. And prove yourself you did. You earned the respect of your troops and your fellow officers. You did not command the powers of fire, but you were still your mother's daughter. In time, you rose as high in the military ranks as a mere human could be expected to. When the rigors of age began to wear upon you, you retired to a villa in the East.

The first few years that you lived near Rana, the harvests were good, and you were able to forget the life you left behind. However, when the Fair Folk attacked the village near your home, you returned to your military ways without a thought, defending your neighbors with the weapons at hand. As you faced the Fair Folk, the Sun called to you. You felt strength course through your old body like you'd never known before. The weapons and armor you had stored as a remembrance appeared upon you in a blaze of light. So armored, and with the glorious white-gold light of the Sun burning around you, you single-handedly met the Fair Folk's charge and turned it.

Roleplaying Hints: You hated the saying "destiny shows in the blood" as a youth because you felt it meant your destiny would be a humble one. The Immaculate Order says that the Dragon-Blooded are the closest to the Immaculate Dragons, the closest to spiritual perfection. But with your Exaltation, your heart soared, and a fire burned within you as you recognized your true destiny. You are the Chosen of the Unconquered Sun. You now see the Terrestrial Exalted for what they are. They are heroes and villains, fathers, mothers, children, leaders, followers, all the many diverse things a people can be. But they are a people that have lost their way in the world. The conceit of the Realm was to make the people dependent on it. You feel your primary task is to guide others with your wisdom, to help them to become more able to care for themselves. The true threat comes the Wyld. The Fair Folk are like fire, beautiful, but dangerous. The Fair Folk that value Creation are in the minority, but either way they're a threat.

Image: Fire Orchid is an old woman who wears her age as a badge of honor, rather than as confining chains. Her red hair is heavily streaked with gray, but she moves with the strength and stamina of a youth. She proudly bears the scars of countless battles fought both before and after her Exaltation.

Equipment: Reinforced breastplate, straight sword, short sword

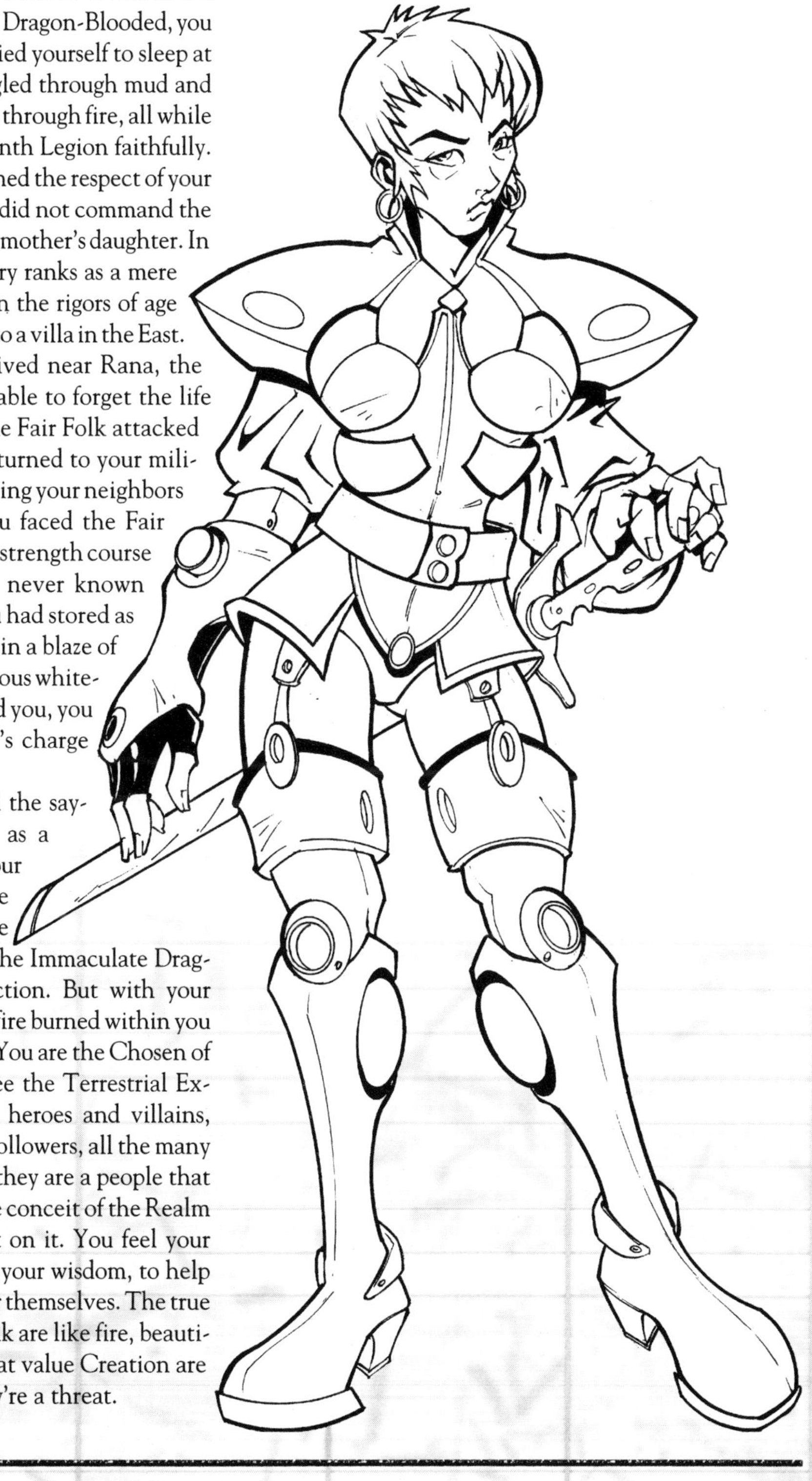

EXALTED

Name: FIRE ORCHID
Player:
Caste: ZENITH
Concept: RETIRED GENERAL
Nature: VISIONARY
Anima:

Attributes

Strength	●●●○○	Charisma	●●●○○	Perception	●●●●○
Dexterity	●●●○○	Manipulation	●●○○○	Intelligence	●●●●○
Stamina	●●●○○	Appearance	●●○○○	Wits	●●●○○

Abilities

Dawn		Zenith		Twilight	
■ Archery	●●○○○	■ Endurance	●●●○○	□ Craft	○○○○○
□ Brawl	○○○○○	■ Performance	●●●●○	□ Investigation	○○○○○
□ Martial Arts	●○○○○	■ Presence	●●○○○	□ Lore	●●○○○
■ Melee	●●●○○	■ Resistance	●●●○○	□ Medicine	○○○○○
□ Thrown	○○○○○	■ Survival	●○○○○	□ Occult	○○○○○

Night		Eclipse		Specialties	
□ Athletics	●○○○○	■ Bureaucracy	●○○○○	□	○○○○○
■ Awareness	●●○○○	□ Linguistics	●●○○○	□	○○○○○
□ Dodge	●●●○○	■ Ride	●○○○○	□	○○○○○
□ Larceny	○○○○○	□ Sail	○○○○○	□	○○○○○
□ Stealth	●○○○○	□ Socialize	○○○○○	□	○○○○○

Advantages

Backgrounds

Background	
RESOURCES	●●●○○
CONTACTS	●●○○○
ALLIES	●●○○○
	○○○○○
	○○○○○
	○○○○○
	○○○○○
	○○○○○
	○○○○○
	○○○○○

Name	Cost	Name	Cost
WHIRLING ARMOR-DONNING PRANA	2/TURN	FURY-INCITING PRESENCE	8, 1W
HAUBERK-SUMMONING GESTURE	5	HEROISM ENCOURAGING PRESENCE	10, 1W
RESPECT COMMANDING ATTITUDE	5	OX-BODY TECHNIQUE	SPEC
UNRULY MOB DISPERSING REBUKE	8, 1W	EXCELLENT STRIKE	1/DIE
ROUT-STEMMING GESTURE	5, 1W	GOLDEN ESSENCE BLOCK	1/2 DICE

Weapons

STRAIGHT SWORD
SPD 6 ACC 7 DMG 6L PRY 7
SHORT SWORD
SPD 6 ACC 6 DMG 5L PRY 4

Willpower

● ● ● ● ● ○ ○ ○ ○ ○
□ □ □ □ □ □ □ □ □ □

Virtues

Compassion ●●○○○ □□□□□
Temperance ●●○○○ □□□□□
Conviction ●●●○○ □□□□□
Valor ●●○○○ □□□□□

Anima

Health

Soak
B 9 L 8 A 7
-2 MOBILITY PENALTY

-0	□■■■■
-1	□□□■■
-2	□□■■■
	□□■■■
-4	□
Incapacitated	□

Essence

● ● ● ○ ○ ○

Personal 14 |
Peripheral 35 |
Committed

Limit Break

□ □ □ □ □ □ □ □ □ □

Virtue Flaw

HEART OF FLINT

Experience

Wind

Quote: *No soul is Exalted by birth, but by its deeds in this life.*

Prelude: From an early age, you wanted to walk the Realm as part of the search for new Immaculate Texts and artifacts of the First Age. As a novice in the Immaculate Order, you befriended mortal and Dragon-Blooded alike. In particular, you befriended and learned from Kirin, from the House of V'neef, who taught you to fight, and Gentle Song, a woman of grace and keen mind, who helped you understand the Immaculate teachings. With these two companions, you achieved your goal to walk the Realm.

A small party from your order, including Kirin and Gentle Song, traveled to the city of Gethamane. It was an ancient place, a city of the First Age, now inhabited by folk who fled the Great Contagion and the advance of the Fair Folk long ago. As you slept in the city, you could sense a presence nearby. By night, screaming awakened you. Investigation revealed a dismembered body and a shadowy figure cloaked in feathers close at hand. When given the opportunity, you approached the mysterious young man without thinking. Your first meeting was interrupted by the approach of Kirin. Afterward, your sleep was troubled by images of the pale man in the feathered cloak. The longer you stayed in Gethamane, the more wary the locals became. On the fifth night of your stay, the Anathema woke you, preventing you from reaching for your sword with a grip like steel. Your second meeting was interrupted by a scream from Gentle Song. You raced to her aid, your visitor close behind. You discovered her in the grip of a monster that filled you with a deep loathing. White and golden light flared all around you, and you struck at the creature, wounding it. With the aid of Kirin and the feathered visitor, you dispatched the thing. In the silence that followed, a thunderous voice and blinding light filled the room. "In the light, the truth will be revealed to you, my son," spoke the Unconquered Sun. When the light faded, you saw Kirin and Gentle Song staring at you in shock. You followed Raiton, your pale new ally, into the night, knowing that you must escape before the Realm's hounds came for you.

Roleplaying Hints: "The soul is not Exalted through birth, but through the journey of life, of which birth is but a single step." These words hold new wisdom for you since your Exaltation. From your birth, you were taught that all Exalted but the Dragon-Blooded were Anathema. Since your rebirth, you have learned the truth. You have learned that the Celestial Exalted were betrayed and struck down by the Terrestrial Exalted, who seized the Realm for their own. You learned that the Solar Exalted are returning. And you learned that you must bring the truth to the people and to the world. The people of the world are a part of the gods' plans for Creation. The gods chose people and granted them the power to fight their enemies, to cast them out of Creation. They empowered the Exalted to guard the world from danger, to rule wisely and well. And you still seek to learn, to discover the secrets of all Exalted and the lost knowledge of the First Age.

Image: Despite turning his back on the Immaculate Order, Wind has not changed his style of dress or hair. He continues to wear the robes of a monk, though the insignia of the Immaculates has been replaced with the sign of the Unconquered Sun. Wind keeps his head shaved as a mark of humility and to allow as much of the Sun's light to shine upon it as possible.

Equipment: Slashing sword, sleeping mat, monk's robes and sandals, alms bowl, walking staff

EXALTED

Name: WIND
Player:
Caste: ZENITH

Concept: MONK
Nature: JUDGE
Anima:

Attributes

Strength	●●●●○	Charisma	●●○○○	Perception	●●●○○
Dexterity	●●●●○	Manipulation	●●○○○	Intelligence	●●●○○
Stamina	●●●○○	Appearance	●●●○○	Wits	●●●○○

Abilities

Dawn

□	Archery	○○○○○
□	Brawl	○○○○○
■	Martial Arts	●●●○○
■	Melee	●●●○○
□	Thrown	○○○○○

Zenith

■	Endurance	●●●○○
■	Performance	●○○○○
■	Presence	●●○○○
■	Resistance	●●●○○
■	Survival	●○○○○

Twilight

□	Craft	○○○○○
□	Investigation	○○○○○
■	Lore	●●○○○
□	Medicine	○○○○○
■	Occult	●●○○○

Night

■	Athletics	●●○○○
□	Awareness	●○○○○
□	Dodge	●●●○○
□	Larceny	○○○○○
□	Stealth	○○○○○

Eclipse

□	Bureaucracy	●○○○○
□	Linguistics	●●○○○
□	Ride	○○○○○
□	Sail	○○○○○
□	Socialize	●○○○○

Specialties

□		○○○○○
□		○○○○○
□		○○○○○
□		○○○○○
□		○○○○○

Advantages

Backgrounds

MENTOR	●●○○○
ALLIES	●●○○○
RESOURCES	●●○○○
CONTACTS	●○○○○
	○○○○○
	○○○○○
	○○○○○
	○○○○○
	○○○○○
	○○○○○

Name	Cost
OX-BODY TECHNIQUE	SPEC
DURABILITY OF OAK MEDITATION	1/2 DICE
IRON SKIN CONCENTRATION	3, 1W
ARMOR OF VIRTUE TECHNIQUE	3

Name	Cost
FIVEFOLD ARMOR OF VIRTUE TECHNIQUE	5
STRIKING COBRA TECHNIQUE	3
SERPENTINE EVASION	3
EXCELLENT STRIKE	1/DIE
HUNGRY TIGER TECHNIQUE	1
ONE WEAPON, TWO BLOWS	3

Weapons

SLASHING SWORD
SPD 9 ACC 8 DMG 6L PRY 8

Willpower

● ● ● ● ● ● ○ ○ ○ ○
□ □ □ □ □ □ □ □ □ □

Virtues

Compassion ●●●●○ □□□□□
Temperance ●●○○○ □□□□□
Conviction ●●○○○ □□□□□
Valor ●●○○○ □□□□□

Anima

Health

Soak

B 3 L 1 A 0

-0	□■■■■
-1	□□□□■
-2	□□■■■
	□□■■■
-4	□
Incapacitated	□

Essence

● ● ● ○ ○ ○

Personal 15 |
Peripheral 37 |
Committed

Limit Break

□ □ □ □ □ □ □ □ □ □

Virtue Flaw

COMPASSIONATE MARTYRDOM

Experience

APPENDIX II
OTHER NOTABLE ZENITH CASTE

VALEBA VISION-TOUCHED

Valeba Vision-Touched was born into a heretical cult, at least from the perspective of the Immaculate Order. His family had always provided a priest of the Sun to those who remained faithful in the surrounding region. Like his father before him, he was expected to uphold the traditions of his long-dead faith. Unlike his father, he questioned the rituals. Valeba saw empty words and meaningless ritual where there was supposedly praise for the Unconquered Sun. Complacency and fear had cooled the people's hearts, and the members of his cult only went through the motions because their parents had.

His family moved constantly through the region as Valeba was growing up. Though the surface reason was to avoid detection by the representatives of the Realm, Valeba secretly believed that his was because of his father's unconscious discomfort with his given role, with the role that would be Valeba's. Despite his misgivings, Valeba was a dutiful son. He learned the rites his father taught him, and when the time came, he bent his knee to the makeshift altar to receive the blessing of the priesthood. But when the ceremony reached its completion, the golden light that surrounded the altar and the would-be priest stunned both father and son. In the rapid series of visions that assailed Valeba, the young man rediscovered the truth and the power of the Unconquered Sun. Now known Valeba Vision-Touched, the young priest found new purpose. With his spirit bolstered by his visions, Valeba began to share his prophecies with those around him. He spoke first to his family, then to his congregation, but as his fame grew, Valeba began to travel more widely.

Journeying in a ever-widening area of the South to avoid the forces of the Immaculate Order, Valeba Vision-Touched has become both prophet and hero to many of

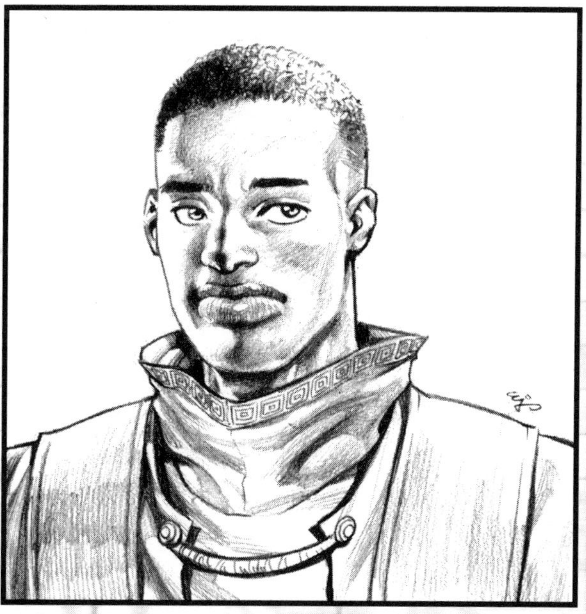

those he encounters. Using skills developed as a youth to avoid imperial forces, he stays in each town he encounters for as long as he can. While in each town, he acts as teacher, instructing the inhabitants in the ways of the Unconquered Sun and the mysteries of the First Age, and as judge, mediating disputes and seeking out the unrighteous and punishing them. Even after he leaves a town, Valeba remains in constant contact, sending written and verbal messages via volunteer runners to encourage and advise his ever-growing flock.

Physically, Valeba is unimpressive. However, he maintains himself and his belongings in a manner befitting a priest of the Unconquered Sun. He accepts donations from his flock to support his way of life but returns any gifts that would cause the giver to go without. Valeba wears white robes decorated with gold-colored threads, which he keeps impeccably clean. His armor and weapons are kept in a constant state of repair, and he will not hesitate to use them in the cause of justice. Valeba is nearly always accompanied by a small group of faithful who serve as assistants in exchange for his teachings.

Bittersea Blackfalcon

The mysterious Bittersea Blackfalcon was born and raised in a tiny shadowland in the West. Her natural beauty was recognized at a young age, and the slender blonde was taken to the master's palace to serve as a dancing girl. Though she dreaded her fate, she had natural skill, learned quickly and excelled at her assigned trade. Before she had reached full womanhood, her incomparable ability had earned her much favor with the lord of the land.

As she grew, she earned a quiet reputation for kindness. As a favorite, and living, servant of a deathknight, she was given all she could desire and more. Comfortable lodging, beautiful clothes and bountiful food were all hers without the asking. However, she had little need to eat and squirreled away her extras. When she was allowed to roam the town, she shared what she could with those who needed it most. Through these small acts of compassion, Bittersea gained a loyal following of friends. Bittersea continued to grow into an adult, and her features matured into a beauty that would have been considered extremely striking elsewhere in the Realm. The somber nature of her surroundings, however, was such that she never realized her beauty or the effect she had on others.

Bittersea Blackfalcon's Exaltation came during a Festival of the Dead. The shadowland in which she lived had recently fought off an incursion by the imperial armies; to celebrate, the land's Abyssal master threw a festival. Some of the living were rewarded for their efforts in the battle by being blessed with undeath, while others were to be slain to replace the walking dead destroyed in the conflict. She danced for the entertainment of her lord while living

citizens of the region were brought before him to receive his gift. As she watched, Bittersea felt a burning within her. The helplessness that had driven her life was being burned away by something new. The woman found herself surrounded with golden flame as she came to the defense of her neighbors. She allowed those who sought death to receive the gift offered by the land's dark master, but those who sought life, she guarded jealously.

A tense standoff ensued. White-gold light opposed inky blackness. For a time, it appeared that the newly reborn Zenith Caste would have to destroy her home to save it. The lord of the land was a crafty noble and had no desire to see his realm crumble. The Abyssal of the shadowland recognized that darkness cannot fully exist without light and spoke at length with Blackfalcon. In the end, it was agreed that those who wished to served the Sun would be allowed to remain in the land and in the protection of Bittersea. However, it was also agreed that Bittersea would turn her powers to aid the master of the land against the forces of the Realm. Blackfalcon believed the Realm to be greater threat and one she had much less influence over, so she remained in the land of the dead, an ever-growing light, accompanied by an ever-growing shadow.

Hetman Lenurel

A native of the Hundred Kingdoms, Lenurel was destined for leadership even before he received the touch of the Unconquered Sun — or perhaps the two destinies were always tied. Lenurel seemed to thrive where others struggled to survive, and those who followed his advice thrived right along with him. Lenurel was blessed with a keen mind and a remarkable insight. As he grew from boy, to teen, to man, it seemed only natural that he receive